Camilla Isley is ̶ ̶ ̶ ̶ ̶ ̶ ̶ ̶ ̶ she quit her job to follow her husband on an adventure abroad.

She's a cat lover, coffee addict, and shoe hoarder. Besides writing, she loves reading—duh!—cooking, watching bad TV, and going to the movies—popcorn, please. She's a bit of a foodie, nothing too serious.

A keen traveler, Camilla knows mosquitoes play a role in the ecosystem, and she doesn't want to starve all those frog princes out there, but she could really live without them.

You can find out more about her here: **camillaisley.com** and by following her on Twitter or Facebook.

@camillaisley
facebook.com/camillaisley

By The Same Author

Romantic Comedies

Standalones
I Wish for You
A Sudden Crush

First Comes Love Series
Love Connection
I Have Never
A Christmas Date

New Adult College Romance

Just Friends Series
Let's Be Just Friends
Friend Zone
My Best Friend's Boyfriend
I Don't Want To Be Friends

A Christmas Date

(A Festive Holidays Romantic Comedy)

FIRST COMES LOVE

BOOK 3

CAMILLA ISLEY

This is a work of fiction. Names, characters, businesses, places, events and incidents either are products of the author's imagination or are used fictitiously. Any resemblance to actual events or locales or persons, living or dead, is entirely coincidental.

Dedication

To all sisters who bicker a little at Christmas…

One

Christmas Is Coming

"Your mother called again," my assistant, Melanie, informs me as soon as I step foot into my office. "Third time this week."

I sit behind my desk and peek at the calendar placed next to my unopened laptop.

Tuesday, December 11

Only Tuesday and we're already on the third call of the week.

Bodes well.

"I'll call her back when I have a minute," I tell Melanie. "Anything else?"

Still standing on the threshold, she shifts on her feet, uncomfortable.

"Come on, I won't shoot the messenger," I promise her.

"Right, because she's asked me to read you this, word for word."

From the way Melanie is cowering, it can't be good. I lean back in my white leather chair, cross my hands in my lap, and sigh. "Go ahead."

"Nikki," she intones, "I spent thirty-five hours in excruciating pain to bring you into this world, and the least I deserve after nurturing you in a loving home for years is for my daughter to return my calls, especially at Christmas. I've already set my expectations very low, as I wouldn't presume you could pick up the phone and call your mother of your own free will…"

I grip the armrests of my chair until my knuckles turn white. "Can you skip the guilt tripping part and get to the core of the message?"

Melanie looks up at me. "Yeah, sure." Her eyes shift back to the note, and she scrolls through the words for what feels like ages. "Ah, yes," she finally sighs. "She demands to know when you'll be heading home for Christmas, how long you're staying, and if you're bringing someone."

I hate the holidays. And I hate when Mom uses the absent-daughter trope to shame me into doing what she wants. But what I hate the most is the two combined. And Christmas is the most inescapable holiday of all.

My stupid boss, along with millions of other idiots scattered around the planet, loves Christmas. So what does the prick do every year? He closes shop, forcing everyone to go on vacation. Which means that every December, without fail, I'm trapped visiting my family in Connecticut for too many days.

Even worse, this year Christmas falls on a Tuesday, meaning the agency will stay closed from the twenty-second to the twenty-ninth. Nine sanity-challenging days of hell in total. And my mother knows, and she's been on my case for a month now to make sure she'll get me for as many of those nine days as she can.

This must be punishment for something terrible I did in a past life, I swear.

I exhale. "I'll call her back when I have a minute."

Melanie is giving me the no-you-won't stink eye, but I have my mean boss poker face on, so she keeps quiet.

"Is that all?" I ask.

"Err, no. You have lunch with your sister today."

And my day isn't getting any better.

"I'll have to reschedule," I say, shuffling the notes from the morning's meetings. "Can you call Julia and tell her?"

"I could have... if you'd asked me this morning. But she's been waiting for you in the lobby for twenty minutes."

"What?!" I stare at my watch.

Half-past noon, already. Where did the morning go?

Well, no way out, then.

***

"Jules," I greet my younger, blessed with all the good Moore genetics, sister.

With natural blonde hair, blue eyes, and an angel face, she's the opposite of my dark hair, brown eyes, and sharp features. When people want to pay me a compliment, they tell me I'm interesting, unique, strong... never beautiful. Julia has always had the pretty-sister crown firmly glued to her head. Ever since we were babies, and her golden curls made her look like a cherub out of a painting. Even as a toddler, I was unimpressive.

"Nikki," Julia shrieks, pulling me into a hug in the middle of the lobby. Without leaving me time to react, she grabs my hand and drags me out of the building. "I can't believe we're really having lunch! I was sure you'd cancel at the last minute. When Melanie didn't call this morning, I was kind of surprised."

Guess the absent-sister guilt technique is another trait she inherited from our mother. And, okay, I'm not the best at keeping engagements... Or calling, or texting... And it's not that I don't love Jules... It's only that being around my baby sister is so hard sometimes...

3

"About that." I avoid looking at her by buttoning up the collar of my coat against the freezing air. "Can we go somewhere nearby? I have to get back to the office soon."

Hidden behind a curtain of flying hair, I watch as Jules struggles not to let her smile falter.

"Sorry," she says, linking our arms and dragging me to the edge of the curb to hail a cab. "I've already picked a place, and Paul is meeting us there."

A cab screeches to a halt in front of us seconds later, thankfully distracting Julia and buying me enough time to compose my features. Otherwise, my expression would've given me away. If being around Jules is hard, the combo Julia *and* Paul leans dangerously close to unbearable. Worse than family and holidays.

I open the cab's rear door and settle on the black leather seat. Not because I've accepted my fate, but because I really need to sit before I fall down. Julia squeezes in next to me.

Once the cab pulls into traffic, I casually ask, "If you're having lunch with your boyfriend, why do you need me to tag along? Don't you guys want to be alone?"

I'm still hoping I can escape. I could hop off the taxi at the next traffic light and grab a hot dog from a street cart on the way back... It'd be so easy. A perfect, quick, sans Jules & Paul lunch.

"Don't be silly," Julia says, laughing as she crushes my getting-out-of-lunch fantasy. "Paul loves you as a sister, just as much as I do."

Ah.

Whoever said words hurt more than actions was so right. I focus on the tall city buildings sweeping by, fighting a losing battle with the lump in my throat. I don't utter a word for the rest of the fifteen-minute trip, and follow Julia out of the cab as it pulls up in front of... *No!*

I stare transfixed at the retro diner that used to be my and Paul's special place, now *their* special place. Behind the glass walls, Paul is already seated in a red vinyl booth, waiting for us at our usual table, now also *theirs*.

Nuh-uh, I don't think I can go in there. My feet are glued to the concrete. I can't move.

That is, until Jules pulls my hand forward, saying, "Come on, Nik, it's freezing out here."

She drags me the few steps to the door and pushes it open, pulling me into the past. Back to almost ten years ago when it was just Paul and me, when Julia was still in high school and living at home. Out of my life, never into his.

Big Mama hasn't changed since then: the black and white tiled floor, the red booths near the windows, and the row of metal stools with cushions of the same red vinyl along the bar on the other side. Even the air smells the same: of burgers and fries, vanilla, and coffee that never stops coming.

Paul and I have been friends since freshman year in college; we were both majoring at NYU in marketing, with a minor in design. Before we officially met—thanks to the Typography professor pairing us for the course project—I'd seen him around campus. It was impossible not to notice Paul. Blond, tall, with broad shoulders and a square jaw, he was a poster child for all-American wholesome handsomeness.

But before academic requirements forced us together, the idea of talking to him never crossed my mind, even if we shared almost every class. I didn't dislike him per se; I'd simply dismissed him as way out of my league, and someone who my parents would approve of too much.

They do, by the way.

I'm not sure how Big Mama became our regular meeting place. It could've been because here we could eat breakfast at any hour, or because the coffee was cheap and never ran out, or because the place was open 24/7... It just happened as our friendship happened: naturally.

One conversation with Paul was enough to make me go back on all my prejudices about him. Paul Collins wasn't just a pretty face in preppy clothes; he was smart, and fun, but also a creative genius—in short, a boy even more out of my league. Not that it mattered, as he had a girlfriend at the time: Marie, who, I suspect, barely tolerated our collaboration and following friendship.

For a long time, I believed Paul and I would be one of those couples who finally come together after an unfortunate mix of missed connections and bad timing. When he broke up with Marie, I was in another relationship, and when that ended, he'd started dating someone else. Then his first job out of college was in Chicago, where he lived for three years while I stayed in New York. But when he came back to the city single and called me to grab a coffee at our old spot, I thought, *This is it, we're finally going to happen.*

Little did I know that day would turn into the worst of my life instead. Whenever I try to pin down exactly how all my dreams of a future with Paul were crushed, I can't. My brain, probably suffering from a bad case of PTSD, has erased the details to protect me. All I remember is that while I was with Paul, Julia, who had also moved to the city by then, called me with some stupid emergency and joined us at the diner. Well, that was enough to erase me from

Paul's dating map forever. If I'd ever been there at all.

From the moment Jules sat down next to me, it was as if I didn't exist anymore. Conversation just sparked between them, it was like there were fireworks coming across the table, while I remained invisible. That day, I officially became the old college friend who had introduced Paul to the love of his life. Big Mama ceased to be our special place, and instead became the special spot where they met.

Ten years of shared history wiped out by one of Julia's smiles.

Never, with any of Paul's previous girlfriends, had I experienced that sense of terrible loss, of a future that now could never be. Because even if they broke up, he would be my sister's ex: permanently off-limits. Sadly, that's also when I realized Paul meant more to me than an old crush or a romantic fantasy about a friend. I was in love with him. Had been for years. But on the same day I understood the depth of my feelings for him, they became forbidden.

As far as I know, Julia had no idea Paul wasn't just a friend for me. And by the time I figured myself out, they were already dating. Too late for me to call dibs on him. And no matter how much it hurt to sit silently by and watch them fall in love, I couldn't bring myself to ruin their relationship. I cared too much about both of them.

Now, as I walk back onto the crime scene, I'm all jitters.

Why has Julia dragged me here? Why are we having lunch with Paul? Let's hope at least it'll be quick. I mean, they both have jobs to go back to. Don't they?

The moment we sit, a server comes with menus. Like the diner, the menus haven't changed; the same big, laminated sheets barely legible through the years of grease that has seeped into the plastic. Not that I need to check the menu. I know what I'm getting, and also what Paul's ordering.

I leave my menu on the table and stare at Jules as she tries to decipher the writing under the dirty plastic to find something allowed by whatever diet she's following at the moment—not that she needs one.

When the server comes back, she turns to Paul first. He orders the fluffy pancakes, as I knew he would. Then, looking at me, he adds, "French toast with berries and cream?"

I can't help but smile and nod. He remembered.

"And you, honey?" Paul asks Julia. "What are you getting?"

All eyes are now on my sister.

"I'll take... Mmm..." Jules purses her lips. "The chicken salad without the chicken, eggs, bacon, and onions. Leave the dressing on the side, please."

Our server raises an eyebrow but doesn't comment, just writes Julia's order on her pad.

Paul sighs—half-amused, half-exasperated—and orders a round of Bloody Marys for everyone. Julia asks for hers to be virgin.

When the server's gone, Jules turns toward Paul with a complicit smile. "Should we tell her now?"

Paul shifts in his booth. "Maybe we should wait for our drinks."

"Tell me what?" I ask.

My sister smiles at me. "We have some very special news to share, and we wanted to do it here."

I don't like how this sounds. I look at Paul for reassurance, but he only shrugs in response. At once, my palms go clammy with sweat.

"This is where we met," Jules continues, "and if it weren't for you, it would've never happened."

Don't I know!

"So it seemed the perfect place to tell you..." My sister pauses for effect. "Are you ready?"

No!

Can I say, no, run out of the diner, and never see them again?

I swallow, grimace, and nod.

Julia takes a deep breath and says, "We're engaged!"

Something pulls tight in my chest, and I blab the first thing that comes into my head, "T-to each other?"

"Of course to each other, silly." Having thus handed down my death sentence, Jules launches into a wedding planning rant. "No need to say, you'll be my maid of honor. The main color scheme for the ceremony and reception will be cream and peach. But I'll need your visual expertise to make sure everything is perfect."

"I-I produce commercials," I manage to stutter. "I don't plan weddings."

"Yeah, but you have an eye for setting, wardrobe, photography... You're the ace up my sleeve. We're still debating over two different wedding planners, but as soon as we pick one I'll let you have their contact so we can all coordinate..."

I don't interrupt her a second time. I let her blab on and on about all her wedding ideas while I nod and mmm-hmm every now and then whenever I feel a pause in the conversation requires it. Conversation... more like a monologue. I should be glad my input isn't needed. There's too much of a strong buzz inside my head for me to be able to communicate anyway. Something like the loud ambient interference of a microphone standing too close to the speakers. I'm the microphone, and Jules and Paul's engagement is the amplifier making my brain explode and taking my heart with it.

Two

Blue Christmas

"You think I'm making a mistake?" Jules asks.

Her voice drags me out of the haze I've been in since my sister dropped the bombshell that she and Paul are engaged. I stare up at her, surprised to see we're both in my office. That I'm sitting behind my desk while my sister is perched on it and is eyeing me expectantly. I don't remember paying for lunch, or even if I said goodbye to Paul. Did I congratulate them? I hope my strict, uptight education kicked in at some point, and that I managed to be at least polite, if not overenthusiastic.

I'm not sure why Julia came back uptown with me after we left Big Mama. Or why she followed me all the way to my office. Or why she's now seated on my furniture asking very stupid questions.

"A mistake?" My words come out in a hiss. Julia is marrying Paul; how dare she not thank her lucky stars? "What do you mean, a mistake?"

"Only that Paul is so predictable sometimes, don't you think?" Jules doesn't let me answer before she continues. "Take the way he proposed. He made a romantic dinner at home with candlelight and roses and popped the question after dessert."

Red. I see red, and I'm not sure I can keep the anger out of my voice as I ask, "And what would a worthy proposal have entailed?"

"Something more original... More special. Take Amanda's boyfriend." Amanda is her best friend. "Joshua asked her on the summit of a wild mountain after they'd struggled to the top together. Paul's proposal was so cliché by comparison."

"I'm pretty sure that if Paul ever asked you to go rock-climbing, you'd dump him on the spot."

Jules shrugs. "Fair enough, but you're missing the point."

"Enlighten me."

"Sometimes I think Paul is a bit, you know, *boring*. Take his looks, for example, blond hair, blue eyes, square jaw... He's just so WASP-y; even his job is so proper and expected..."

I'm trying really hard not to start yelling what an ungrateful, spoiled brat she is. "I'm curious, how would a non-boring man look?"

Julia stares at the ceiling with a dreamy expression. "Don't you ever dream of an adventure with a tall, dark stranger? Someone with smoldering green eyes and full lips, and danger written all over his face. Someone who speaks Italian and doesn't own a car."

"And how would he get around? On the subway?"

The last time my sister took the subway, I was still in college.

"Ew, no. He would ride a bike, of course. One of those big, black monsters... We're talking about the kind of guy who sweeps you off your feet with just one look, who can make you fall hard and fast. Someone mysterious, intriguing..."

"And what occupation would this dangerous stranger have, since marketing is clearly so out of style with you?" I ask, even if I agree that Paul's job isn't exactly exciting. I've no clue why he decided to waste all his creativeness to go work in the driest, most Corporate America branch of marketing the city has to offer.

"You didn't get offended, did you?" Jules says. "When I said Paul's job is boring, I didn't mean yours, too. You do completely different things."

Her disrespect of my profession is the least of my concerns at the moment.

"Not at all," I say.

"Anyway," she continues, unfazed. I suspect I could've said I was mortally offended, and I would've gotten the same reaction. "My stranger would have to be some kind of struggling artist, someone who lives paycheck to paycheck, and who appreciates everything he has because he doesn't know if he's going to still have it tomorrow."

"So you basically want to marry a penniless, unemployed artist, who'd propose to you on top of a big rock with a plastic ring because he can't afford a real diamond?"

"I never said marry, I only said I'd like one last adventure. Is that so wrong?"

"I don't know. You're the one about to walk down the aisle."

I must've been scowling more than I realized, because Jules goes on the defensive. "No, you're right. I'm just being silly. But it's hard to think I'm done with first dates and first kisses… That Paul will be *it* for me for the rest of my life."

Considering the last few disastrous first dates I went on, I count Julia lucky she won't ever have to go on another one. "First dates are overrated, trust me."

She smiles. "Maybe you're right. But this is all so new; it's normal for me to have some wedding jitters, isn't it?"

I've had enough. "Listen, Jules, I don't mean to be rude, but I really have a ton of work to do…"

"Sorry." Julia hops off the desk. "I've already stolen too much of your time. Thank you for talking me down." She pulls on her coat. "I'll send you the wedding planner's contact as soon as I've picked one…"

"Whatever you need." I hug her goodbye and usher her out. "You know the way, right?"

"Yeah." She gives me another quick hug and goes.

I don't watch her get to the elevators; I shut the door to my office and pull down all the blinds. Back behind my desk, I drop my head on its cold surface and wait for the tears to come. Only they won't. After holding back for too long, my body is wired to resist and refuses to let go.

For the rest of the afternoon I stare blankly at my screen, finishing none of the work I was supposed to do—namely, the final revision of a lipstick commercial that starts shooting soon. A high-end gig with A-list models and a top-notch director. I just scroll through the art boards, casting pictures, and wardrobe selection without really seeing any of it. By the time Melanie knocks on my door to tell me she's leaving for the night, I've no idea what the plan is for the shoot the day after tomorrow.

Ah, hell. I decide to follow Melanie out. Take the night off, process the blow, and come back in the morning as good as new. The engagement doesn't really change anything. They already live together… Marriage won't make their relationship any better… Only more permanent… More unbreakable…

Kids are coming next, a vicious voice whispers inside my head.

As I walk out of my building, I try to imagine what a

Jules & Paul baby would look like. Gorgeous, for sure, with blonde hair and blue eyes... Perfect, really. They're going to have perfect babies, to live in their perfect house, after their perfect wedding.

Despite the biting cold, my feet refuse to walk me to the subway station. Instead, I wander the streets of New York surrounded by a frenzied holiday crowd. Revoltingly cheery people going about their jolly business amidst colorful shopping windows and those sickening Christmas tunes coming out of a thousand speakers hidden everywhere in the city.

A couple in front of me stops to kiss under a mistletoe wreath. Disgusted, I side-step past them, only to be assailed by a blinding display of red and green lights. Between the music, the lights, the colors, and the crowd, my head starts spinning. It seems like the whole city is bearing down on me. I need to get somewhere dark and quiet, *now!*

As I quicken my pace, my eyes catch on a shop window without even a hint of red or green, or of a single Christmas decoration. Instead of sickening jingle bells, modern lounge music is drifting out from under the glass door.

On impulse, I walk in.

An Asian guy with shoulder-length, platinum-blond hair welcomes me with an apologetic smile. "Sorry, dear, but we're almost closing. Did you have an appointment?"

An appointment? I take in the twin rows of black leather chairs in front of floor-to-ceiling mirror walls and realize I've walked into a hair salon.

"No, sorry," I say. "I just needed a break from all this holiday madness, and your place was so..."

The guy nods understandingly. "We pride ourselves in being the anti-Christmas types. So, my darling fellow

Grinch, having a bad day?"

"Horrible." I walk toward one of the chairs. "Can I sit here for five minutes and breathe some un-festive fresh air?"

"Sure, sure." He gestures for me to sit, and I don't know if it's out of professional habit, but he starts combing his fingers through my hair. "Such a blank canvas," he says, pulling apart a few locks. "When was the last time you had it trimmed?"

"Honestly? I don't remember. It's been a while."

I like my hair as it is: long, dark, straight. And I haven't changed my style in forever. If it ain't broke…

"And are you feeling adventurous today?"

"No, *no!* Not at all."

I make to get up, but my host keeps me in place with a gentle pressure on my shoulders.

"Mmm, I'm not sure you've walked in here by chance, darling. Sure you're not ready for a change?"

I'm about to say "no" again, when the question really sinks in. Am I ready for a change? Do I want to keep spending my life pining after my sister's boyfriend—sorry, fiancé?

No.

Do I want to keep dreading the holidays and every visit home?

No.

So, am I ready for a change?

Hell yeah!

I meet the guy's eyes in the mirror.

"That's what I thought." He smiles knowingly. "I work only by appointment, but I will make an exception for you, little bird."

16

"Oh, no. You were about to close, I wouldn't want to make you stay late. I can come back tomorrow."

The stylist gives me a piercing stare through the mirror. "You walk out of that door now, honey, and we both know I'll never see you again."

He's right.

"Okay. Let's do this."

"Great!" He pats my shoulders. "Now, tell me how much of a radical change you want."

I lift my chin. "Make me a new woman."

***

After leaving the salon, I spend the rest of the walk home spying on my reflection in every shop window I pass. I barely recognize myself. Jiang—the genius hairstylist— basically turned me into Jaimie Alexander's secret twin sister. Think Nina Dobrev from the pilot episode of *The Vampire Diaries* to the series finale makeover. Only my new cut is shorter and more radical.

And so bouncy, and so fresh, and so not me.

As I unlock my apartment door, my phone pings with a new text. I drop my bag on the counter, take out the phone, and sag on the couch, exhausted.

What a day!

My fingers are so cold from my stroll around Manhattan that when I try to unlock the phone, the touchscreen almost doesn't recognize them as warm, human flesh. Only after I blow hot air on my fingertips and swipe twice more does it work, and I can read the text.

It's from Blair, my best friend and roommate.

Sorry I haven't been home
in forever

I'll be there in a few minutes

Are you in?

Just got here

Great

I have some big news

Bought champagne to
celebrate

Champagne? Oh gosh, she's getting married, too. Richard proposed. I try to summon some altruistic joy, but I can't. There's only one thought drilling through my skull: I'm going to be single forever and die alone.

Just like that, out of nowhere, the tears come. My chest and shoulders spasm with body-wrenching sobs, and I don't seem to be able to stop the flood.

The frustration, the pain... the bitter jealousy, for my sister, for my best friend... they all come out in a downpour. Oh, gosh, I'm a horrible person who doesn't deserve love. Why would anyone love *me?* I'm dark and grumpy and stubborn—simply, utterly unlovable.

That's how Blair finds me a few minutes later: a

sobbing, self-loathing mess sprawled on the couch.

"Oh my gosh, Nikki." She rushes into the living room, coat still on, dropping a bottle of bubbly on the coffee table, where she sits. "Are you okay?"

I try to speak, but it's difficult when you're crying as hard as I am, so I only shake my head.

Blair does a double take and points at my face, shocked. "Your hair—it's gone! Are you crying about the haircut?"

"Noooooooo," I wail. "S-should I be c-crying about it?"

"No, no!" Blair jumps in to reassure me. "I love it like this! But it's a big transformation… I thought maybe you did it on the spur of the moment, then changed your mind. Is that it?"

I shake my head again.

"So what is it?"

After a few deep breaths, I speak the unspeakable. "Julia and Paul are engaged."

Blair doesn't respond. She removes her coat, kicks off her shoes, and slides onto the couch next to me, taking me into her arms. She pets me and cuddles me as I tell her everything: the lunch at Big Mama, the announcement, Jules' stupid doubts, my lone walk through the streets of Manhattan, and the hair salon.

"Do you really like my hair this way?" I ask at the end.

"Love it!" Blair smiles sincerely.

I hug her tighter. "Distract me. What was your big news?"

Out of the corner of my eye, I catch her throwing a guilty look at the champagne bottle. A thick layer of condensation now covers the dark glass. The wine's got to be warm by now. Great, I ruined her celebration.

"Oh, nothing," she says, brushing my question off.

"Let's talk about it another night."

"You bought the bubbly," I insist. "Don't tell me it's nothing."

She chews on her index nail, undecided.

"Did Richard propose, too?"

"No," Blair says and, still biting her nail, adds, "but he asked me to move in with him."

I try to smile, I really try, but my lower lip starts trembling. I manage an, "I'm so happy for you," before I start sobbing again.

Blair pulls me back into her arms and tries to console me. "It won't be super soon. I told him we would need time to figure things out, and I'm not going anywhere until you're okay. Listen, I know the holidays are hard for you, and I'm here. Richard is going back to England over the break, but I'm staying in the States. We'll go home together, and whenever it gets too hard at your place, you can come and crash in my room, I promise. It'll be just you, me, and Chevron. A girls' club."

I calm down a little. Blair coming home to Connecticut with me is the lifeline I need to survive this Christmas. Knowing she'll be there is the only positive piece of news I've gotten all day. Also, for the first time, I notice Chevron—Blair's semi-golden-retriever dog—didn't come home with her.

"Hey, where did you leave Chevron?"

"At Richard's. I took the subway back. With traffic, it would've taken forever in his car, and it was too cold to walk, even for me."

"Oh, I could've used the extra cuddles."

Chevron is the most empathic and *only* dog I like.

"I thought you were a cat person."

"I am, but Chevron is basically a cat born in the wrong body."

Blair smirks. "If you say so."

"At least when the two of you move out I'll be able to adopt a real cat, body and soul."

The thought almost cheers me up, if not for the mocking voice inside my head announcing, *Ladies and gentlemen, I give you Nikki Moore: single, alone, and crazy cat-less cat lady.*

Three

The Perfect Man for Christmas

The next morning, I arrive at the office super early. Not only to catch up with work, but also to avoid the double-takes and possibly false compliments my impromptu makeover will spur.

I've just finished checking the wardrobe for tomorrow's shoot when Melanie walks in. She stops just inside the door and makes a shocked, "oh-I-walked-into-the-wrong-office" face. Then she blinks, realization dawning. Closing the door behind her, she approaches my desk slowly. "Your hair…"

"Is shorter," I say, making it clear that, no, I don't want to talk about it. "What can I do for you?"

"Your mother called again… I'm running out of excuses…"

"Arrrrrrrrgh…" I let out an exasperated growl and drop my head in my hands.

"Mmm… Are you okay, boss?"

"No, I'm not okay." I lift my head and bang both fists on the desk. Not content, I brush off all the sheets of paper crowding it in a crazed swipe. The documents tumble to the floor, carrying a pen holder and my landline phone with them.

I stare at the mess with a small surge of satisfaction. Melanie, on the other hand, has gone pale.

"Sorry," I say. My reaction was atypical; I've never freaked out in front of her. "I'm not mad at you."

Still wary, my assistant sits in the chair opposite to mine. "Okay, boss, tell me what's going on."

Over the years, I've always strived to maintain a professional relationship with Melanie. But she's been with me from the start, and we've also developed a friendship-with-boundaries. This is one of the times I feel like testing those limits a little.

"It's the holidays and I'm single, while Julia just got engaged…" I skip the "to the love of my life" part, to maintain a shred of credibility in front of my assistant. "My roommate just told me she's moving in with her boyfriend. And in less than two weeks, I'll have to go home and listen to every single one of my relatives ask me why I'm still single. When what they really mean is, 'What's wrong with you? Why does nobody want you?'"

I huff. Aww… it felt good to let it all out.

Melanie absorbs all the personal info like a pro. "Is it the 'single at the holidays' part that bothers you, or is it your family?"

Good question. I don't particularly enjoy being single, and the prospect of dying a crazy cat lady is not very appealing. But why does the anxiety get so much worse near the end of the year? I'm fine with my life eleven months out of twelve, but every December I promptly turn into a train wreck. Does Christmas make being a spinster harder? Or is it the judgment in Aunt Betsy's thin-lipped smiles? The ill-concealed sadness behind my mother's eyes for my "condition?" Or the well-intentioned-but-deeply-insensitive jokes everyone spins me back home?

It's not me. It's them.

"My family," I tell Melanie. "They drive me nuts."

"Well, but that's an easy fix."

"Really? How?"

"You're an executive producer. Produce them."

"What do you mean?"

"There must be a gay best friend—possibly with the looks of Rupert Everett—you can ask to go home with you and pretend to be your boyfriend."

Sometimes I forget my assistant is still basically a child. At twenty-five, she's not jaded enough about life to accept not everything can be solved "Hollywood Style" and end in happily ever after.

Pity happily ever afters don't exist. Some genius in my profession invented them to sell romance to the crowds. That's all.

"Sorry, Mel, but I'm not Julia Roberts and this isn't a movie. No gorgeous gay besties in the picture."

"A straight friend would do, too. Anyone you can ask?"

Ironically, the one male friend I could've felt intimate enough to ask something so embarrassing would've been Paul. Isn't life funny sometimes?

"Not really," I say.

"Well, then hire someone!"

"Are you suggesting I hire a male escort?" And we've moved from *My Best Friend's Wedding* to *The Wedding Date,* maybe she has a thing for Dermot Mulroney. "Are you crazy? I'm not that desperate."

"I was thinking more an actor." She points at my computer. "You have a database full of them right there in front of you; you just have to pick and choose."

"That's even more absurd and unprofessional." To signify that this conversation is finished, I bend forward and start collecting the scattered documents from the floor. "Break's over," I say, pushing up the pen holder.

"All right, boss," Melanie says, getting up. She helps me clean the mess and places my office phone back on the desk, eyeing it meaningfully. "But your mom won't give up, you know?"

Don't I?

***

Another afternoon of staring into space earns me a late night at the office. I wish nothing more than to go home, change into a pair of sweatpants, and watch a silly romcom that will make me cry and despise my life even more. But I can't leave before every minute of tomorrow's shoot is mapped out. And I need to also check the ad sales reports on my holiday commercials and recheck the TV air schedules for the projects I'm following. So I trudge on, even if my eyes keep crossing over the endless Excel sheet lines and columns.

By 8:30 p.m. I'm so exhausted that, when my landline rings, I pick up without thinking.

"Nikki Moore."

"Nikki!" My mother sounds both astounded and utterly ecstatic she's finally cornered me. "I thought I'd get your voicemail. I'm not sure your secretary is passing along all my messages. What are you still doing at the office this late?"

"Working, obviously."

"Work, work, work. You work too much, honey, there's more to life than just work."

I could come up with a million retorts. But if I argue back, the conversation will spiral into a sermon from my mother. A lecture starting with a list of all the important things I'm neglecting, and ending in a praise of the perfect work-life balance Julia has achieved. So, instead of defending my right to be focused on my career, I give her the easy response.

"Mom, you know how busy it gets at the holidays, worst time of the year. I really need to finish up here, so…"

"I'll be quick, then." Now that she has me, she's not going to let me off the hook that easily. "I wanted to know when you're coming home for the break. Julia is coming on the twenty-second."

I peek at the calendar. The twenty-second is the Saturday before Christmas.

"Either then, or on the twenty-third," I say. "I'm sharing a car with Blair, and we haven't made a decision yet."

"But you'll definitely be here by Sunday night."

"Yes."

"And when are you leaving?"

"Not sure yet, Mom." I try to stall before she traps me up there for a full week. "Depends on what my plans for New Year's are."

"Oh, are you going somewhere?"

I twist the cord around my fingers and say, "I could." Which isn't an outright lie. I *could* go on a trip; I'm just not planning to.

"All right, we can settle that once you get home." I think she's finally going to cut me loose when she adds, "So, you've heard about Julia and Paul. Isn't it wonderful news?"

Peachy, I'd say, to keep in tone with the wedding color scheme.

"Yeah, I had lunch with them yesterday."

"Oh, great. So, I was wondering if you wouldn't mind swapping rooms with your sister?"

"And why should I do that?"

"Because your bed is bigger, and since Paul is spending

the holidays with us—"

"WHAT?!"

"Isn't it marvelous? He's almost part of the family now, and it makes sense he'd want to be with us at Christmas."

"And what about *his* family? Don't they want to spend Christmas Day with their son?"

"I think his mom prefers Thanksgiving. Anyway, can I tell Julia she can have your room?"

"No."

"Nikki, don't be unreasonable. You're coming home by yourself, and they're two—they can't sleep in Julia's bunk bed."

The thought of Julia and Paul sleeping—*and doing who knows what else*—in my old bed blinds me with rage. I lost my virginity on that bed with my first boyfriend—senior year, one spring afternoon when both my parents were out. Julia can't have that, too. That bed has a lot of good memories, and I won't let Julia spoil those as well. She's already collected enough pieces of me.

"I'm not by myself," I say on impulse.

"What do you mean?" my mom asks, surprised.

"My boyfriend is coming with me."

And I'm digging myself a deeper grave with every sentence.

"You have a boyfriend? Since when?"

"Yeah, it hasn't been long, but I wanted you all to meet him."

Lie, after lie, after lie.

"Oh, Nikki, you're making me so happy! What's his name? How did you meet?"

"I don't have time to tell you the whole story now, Mom, but don't worry, you'll meet him soon enough."

"Sure. I'll let you go back to work... So many things to organize here. I love you, honey."

"Love you, too, Mom. Bye."

I hang up and drop my head on the desk over my crossed arms.

What have I done?

I should call her back and tell her it's all been a mistake. That Julia can have my man, my dream life, and even my bed. What does it matter, anyway?

Only it *does* matter. I can't spend a week at home, single and pathetic, sleeping in Julia's tiny princess bed while she shares my bed with Paul. Not possible.

I straighten up.

So, where do I find a boyfriend?

I throw a guilty stare at my computer.

No, I couldn't.

What if someone at the office found out?

Impossible.

No one would ever believe I've hired a fake boyfriend off the agency's database.

With a few quick clicks of the mouse, I close the Excel sheet I was studying and access the actors/models database.

A pop-up window prompts me to input filters to narrow down the search. I select "male" and then, before I know what I'm doing, I start creating an avatar of Julia's ideal man.

Eyes: green
Hair: dark
Height: 6'4" and above
Age: |

I'm undecided if I should include only the 30-34 range or expand it to 25-29 and 35-39. What if the perfect man is 29 or 35? I select all three, just to be on the safe side.

Languages: |

I check English and Italian and click Search.

With my heart in my throat, I wait for the results. Does such a man even exist?

The search engine lands three positive hits. Wow. Apparently, there are a lot more tall, dark-haired, Italian-speaking men in New York than I thought.

I open the first profile, and the picture of a beautiful man pops on the screen. I say "beautiful" because it's clear that this male model favors his feminine side. It's in the delicate pout of his lips and the graceful tilt of his head. No one would ever believe he's in love with me.

I close his profile and open the next one.

Jackpot!

Now, if a man could ever be described as dark, smoldering hot, and mysterious, this guy has nailed all three. The headshot is pretty simple: he's staring at the camera straight up, face forward. His wavy black hair is just long enough to be very sexy, as sexy as his full-lipped mouth, and his green eyes are piercing a hole through the screen. Tyra Banks would say he's smizing at the camera.

I study the picture a little longer... His straight nose is sprinkled with freckles that make him cute on top of sexy. And even the line of his neck is masculine and inviting. He is the perfect man. He's my guy.

His other pictures only reinforce my conviction. A profile shot: equally sexy. One of him smiling: heart-melting. And…

Whoa.

The last picture is a black and white bust shot. Mr. Tall, Dark, and Mysterious is wearing jeans and teasingly lifting a tank top to reveal his bare chest while he stares at the camera with a naughty expression—eyes alive with mischief and mouth curled up at one corner in a lopsided grin. The shot takes my breath away. This must be photoshopped; no real person could really have abs and pectorals that sculpted.

Reluctantly, I close the picture and open his profile.

Diego O'Donnell, age twenty-eight. Two years younger than me, but we live in a modern era where a two-year gap a cougar doesn't make. From his CV I see that the guy has done a few lesser gigs on Broadway and has a couple of high-level commercials under his belt. But nothing so big that it'll make him snub my proposal. Mr. O'Donnell still fits the struggling artist profile.

Mmm, let's see where you live.

The address listed on his file is far away enough from Manhattan to tell me he's not swimming in cash.

Good.

Because I need someone just as desperate as me to take this job.

Fueled up by adrenaline, I save his contact on my phone and press Call.

Four

Here Comes Santa Claus

Nothing.

The call goes to voicemail. I try a second time, with the same result, so I decide to try the other number listed on his profile. Maybe a landline?

"Hello?"

The voice is a letdown. Too creaky to match the man in the picture.

"Hello, Mr. O'Donnell?"

"Who?"

"Diego O'Donnell?"

"Oh, you mean Dunk. He's not home."

"You know when he'll be back?"

"Why?" The dude sounds suspicious.

"I'm calling about a job opportunity, something rather urgent. No chance you'd know where I can find him?"

"He could still be downtown. Dunk had a Santa Claus gig tonight, but it should be over by now."

Diego is in Manhattan! I can barely contain my excitement. "Do you remember where the gig was, by any chance?"

"No, sorry, some fancy mall downtown. You want to leave a message?"

"No need, thank you, I'll call back."

I hang up and nibble at one of my nails. Damn. Now that my folly has gained momentum, I can't lose steam. If only that guy remembered the name of the mall...

Let's see if Google can help. A quick "santa claus

wednesday december 12 manhattan mall" search and...
Bingo! There's only one late-evening event today, and the
address is not too far from my office. The program says the
show ends at 9:30 p.m. If I hurry, I might get there just in
time.

***

Fifteen minutes after the scheduled end of the event, I
arrive at the mall worried sick I might've missed him. But,
luckily, there's still a Santa seated in the winter wonderland
booth at the mall's entrance. He's ushering a kid away, who
an elf assistant promptly replaces with the last toddler in
line, depositing the newcomer on Santa's knee.

As Diego listens to the little boy, I observe my mark to
evaluate if he's as good looking in person, or if he's a
cheat—aka a Photoshop-friendly model who doesn't
understand that going to a casting looking half as hot as his
portfolio is a lose-lose approach. But between the fake
beard and fake belly, it's a hard one to call.

Once the kid has expressed all his Christmas wishes and
taken the customary picture, my man stands up.

Mmm. Impressive. At least he didn't lie about his
height.

"I'm getting hella out of here," his lady elf helper says.
"You coming?"

"Nah, gotta get changed first. See ya soon, Jess."

They bump fists and the girl walks away, still wearing
her red, white, and green costume.

In the few seconds I get distracted by watching the elf
leave, Diego has opened a hidden door and is already
disappearing backstage. Whoops. "Excuse me—!" I call.

"Sorry, Miss, the event's over," he says, without sparing

me a second glance. And then he's gone.

What now? I could wait for him to get changed and come back out, but again, I'm impatient. And if I stay too long out here, I might chicken out, call my mom, and surrender my bed to Julia.

Never.

I throw a circumspect look around. No one's monitoring the booth, so I enter Santa World and follow Diego behind the hidden door into a tiny backstage dressing room. There's barely enough space for a locker and a small bench pushed against the opposite wall.

Diego has the upper half of the locker open, which screens him from my view.

"Excuse me?" I repeat.

"Hey." He closes the locker and throws me an angry stare. "This is personnel only."

He's still wearing the fake beard and Santa hat, but the upper part of the red suit is now dangling upside-down from his hips and the belly stuffer is gone, leaving his ripped chest and abs all too visible under a sweat-soaked white T-shirt. With muscles like that, he could win any wet-T-shirt contest.

I tear my eyes away from his chest, saying, "Yeah, I know. But I really needed to talk to you."

"Listen, lady, if your kid has missed his spot, I'm sorry, but it's late and I want to go home. We're doing another event in two days; you can come back then."

"I'm not here to see Santa. I'm here to see you, Mr. O'Donnell."

He starts at that. "How do you know my name?"

"Nikki Moore, nice to meet you. I work at KCU Advertising, and I'd like to talk to you about a job

33

opportunity."

I don't usually name drop, but I need to gain some credibility before I present him with my crazy plan.

"The big agency on Madison Avenue?"

"Yes, but the job wouldn't be for the agency; you'd be working for me. Care to hear me out?"

He shrugs. "Mind if I keep getting changed?"

"No, not at all. Go ahead."

Diego turns around and pulls the wet T-shirt off his back in one fluid motion. I'm momentarily distracted by more male skin than I've seen in a long while. Gosh, even his back is ripped.

"I'm listening," he says, opening the locker again and blocking my ogling feast.

"Mmm, yeah, so." This is harder to explain than I thought. "It'd be an acting job. Nothing scripted... a lot of improv required. Sort of, you know, like a reality show, but with no cameras. And you might think I'm crazy for asking, but you must understand that the holidays can be a difficult period for many people. Single people, I mean. And people with a family that just won't back off, especially if they have a baby sister who's the poster child of perfection in their mother's eyes. You get what I'm saying?"

Back still turned, Diego says, "Not really." He rips off the rest of the Santa suit, rewarding me with an unobstructed view of his buttocks clad in close-fitting white boxer shorts. Mmm, those buns are so inviting I have to force myself not to reach out and squeeze one. Luckily, in a few quick moves, he pulls on a pair of jeans and a sweatshirt, and, closing the locker for good, turns all his attention to me.

For the first time I see his face without the beard, and

one thing is immediately clear: he's no Photoshop user.

He fluffs his hair, which has been plastered to his head by the hat, and grins. "What's the job again?"

Guess there's really no other way to explain it. "I want to hire you to pose as my boyfriend for the holidays."

Diego opens his mouth to protest, but before he can, I stop him. "And before you say 'no,' please note that the pay is very competitive."

"How competitive?

"Five thousand dollars—twenty-five hundred in advance, and the rest at job completion. And our relationship would be strictly professional."

"While I pretend to be your boyfriend?"

"Exactly."

"I'm sorry, but—"

"Wait. Before refusing, please consider that if you say 'yes,' you'd be doing me a real solid, and I'd be happy to return the favor, professionally, of course, in any way you might need."

I saved the best bone for last. A struggling actor would do anything to have someone who matters in the industry owe him one. As expected, this offer gives him pause.

He scratches his head and studies me. "You're serious? This isn't a joke."

I shake my head. "Dead serious."

"And you work for KCU?"

I whip out my business card and present him with incontrovertible proof. "Mmm-hmm."

He eyes the card, thinking. "You guys are big on Super Bowl commercials. You even won an award last year, yeah?"

"Breath mints, that's us."

"Have you already cast this year's ads?"

"No, we start in early January."

"Can you get me a call in?"

"Into the castings, yes, but the rest is up to you. I can't guarantee a part."

A brief nod lets me know he understands. Then, out of the blue, he asks, "Why me?"

The question takes me off guard. I can't exactly say, *"Because I want my sister to rot with jealousy when I bring her dream guy home for Christmas."* He already thinks I'm nuts.

"We haven't worked together in the past, so there wouldn't be a conflict."

Diego keeps his eyes trained on me for the longest time. "Am I the only actor in your agency's database you haven't worked with before?"

What else can I say to convince him? Only one plausible reason I can think of. "No," I admit. "But you were the best-looking one."

I don't even think I'm lying right now.

My answer seems to have satisfied him. He smiles, forcing all the air out of my lungs. Now I get what *breathtaking* means.

Using basic yoga training to steady my respiration, I ask, "Then we have a deal?"

He offers me his hand. "Deal."

After we shake on it, he pulls on his coat and guides me out of the Santa closet.

"So how is this going to work?" he asks once we reach the mall exit.

The cold night air hits us the moment we step outside. It's freezing, and I've already had enough excitement for one day. So I say, "It's late now. Why don't we discuss the details tomorrow over lunch?"

"Okay."

"You'll find a missed call from me on your phone from about an hour ago. I'll text you a place in the morning."

"All right, boss." As he says "boss," Diego winks at me. Then he turns around to climb on a monstrous black bike that he starts with a roar. "See you tomorrow."

I watch him put on a black helmet and speed away into traffic. I can't believe he even has a bike. I really picked the perfect man for the job.

***

The next day, I'm the first to arrive at the restaurant. I've picked a taqueria not too far from my office, but not too close, either. The last thing I need is to run into a colleague while I'm negotiating contract terms with my fake boyfriend.

Wow, I still can't believe I'm doing this, and that someone else has joined me in this crazy plan. I stare at the list of "hot topics" I've printed out, not sure Diego has grasped the full extent of what he agreed to yesterday. Might be my fault for being accidentally-on-purpose vague enough not to scare him away, but today I need to be one hundred percent assertive about what I want out of this deal.

A change of vibe inside the restaurant makes me lift my head. The normal tones of conversation have quieted down to be replaced by intrigued murmurs. At the table next to mine, the two women who've been bitching non-stop about their boss since I got here are now giggling, eyes fixated on the entrance door. I follow their stares, and my gaze lands on Mr. Tall, Dark, and Smoldering Hot.

Hair ruffled up in all directions, Diego is standing on the threshold scanning the tables, presumably to find me, and mostly unaware of the attention he's commanding from the entire room. Clad in a pair of light-washed jeans, a black leather biker jacket, and with the matching black helmet propped under his arm, he's the incarnation of the bad boy in every woman's fantasy.

I wave to attract his attention. He spots me and reaches our high table in a few quick strides—not surprising with that impressive leg span. While he sits opposite me with a quick, "Hello," I steal a glance at the two women sitting next to us and am ridiculously pleased with the vitriolic looks of pure envy stamped on their faces.

Ah, hell. For once I'm not the single lady having lunch alone, I'm the woman dating the hottest guy in the room—possibly the entire New York state—and who cares if I have to shell out a few thousand dollars for the privilege? Money well invested. I can't wait to stick it to my family for once. To have one glorious Christmas before I become the official family spinster forever.

"Hi," I greet him back. "Did you find the place all right?"

"Yeah." Diego settles his helmet on the empty stool between us. "Been here before."

We lock gazes for the first time since he arrived, and for a second, I have to steady myself. Today is a surprisingly bright day for December, and the sun is hitting Diego's face with just the right light, turning his eyes into two sparkly emeralds.

I clear my throat. "Err, great."

Good thing he's not my type at all. I prefer blue eyes

and blonde hair, and guys with a stable job. Guys like Paul, in short. And Diego sits at the opposite end of the male spectrum. At least there won't be any risk of confusion on my part. And I'm sure on his, too. I don't know what kind of woman is his type, but she must be a few leagues above me in the looks department.

"Are you ready to order?" I ask.

"Yeah, I—"

"Hello, I'm Adalynn, and I'll be taking care of you today," an eager-looking girl interrupts us. She's sporting the smile of a server who's just won the table lottery. "Would you like to hear today's specials?"

Diego smiles back at her and says, "Sure."

"Wonderful." From the way she beams, you'd think he'd just agreed to go on a date with her. "Today's special tacos are the lobster with sweet corn, and fried duck with habanero honey. If I may suggest one, the duck is really something special."

"All right." Diego smizes, eyes as mischievous as in his pictures. "The duck one sounds great."

"Excellent choice. And to drink?"

"A beer, please."

After giving him another small smile, she turns toward me, her enthusiasm fading. "And for you?"

"A chicken taco and a Diet Coke, thank you."

"Perfect. I'll be right back with your drinks."

Adalynn isn't kidding; I haven't even struck up the nerve to broach the fake-boyfriend topic when she returns with our drinks. Setting them down, she throws Diego yet another smile and says, "Let me know if you need anything else."

Reluctantly, she walks away, finally leaving us in peace.

"So," I start, a little nervous. "Thanks for meeting me here today." Oh, come on, Nikki. No need to be nervous. Just treat him as any model or actor you would in one of your productions. Yeah, right. I've got this. "I wanted to go over the details of this job before we sign a formal contract... Did you have questions, or would you like to hear me out first?"

Diego leans his elbows on the table. "I might have too many questions. Best if you outline the ABCs first..."

"Oh, okay." I stare at the first item on my list: comp. "As I said, the compensation is a flat five thousand dollar fee, all included." Better remind him why he's here. "As for the specifics of the job, we need to script the basics: how we met, first date, a few cute anecdotes... stuff like that. And we have to familiarize ourselves with each other to improv the rest. Our interactions must be as natural as possible, and that's why I thought..." I hope he swallows this without protest. "...you should move in with me."

His eyebrows shoot high into his forehead. "Move in with you?"

"Yeah. We have to act as if we've known each other for a couple of months, at the very least." If I'm doing this, I'm doing it right. "I have to learn your tells, you have to learn mine, and living together is exactly the crash course we need. You would have your own room, of course." *Once I convince Blair to let you sleep in her bed, anyway.* But she's moving out soon, so it shouldn't be too hard for her to crash at Richard's until Christmas.

"You're a bit paranoid, you know? We don't need all that preparation to pass for a couple for one dinner."

"One dinner?"

"Yeah, the Christmas meal? Isn't that what we were

talking about?"

"I'm not paying you five thousand dollars to have *one meal* with my family. You have to come with me to my hometown in Connecticut for a *week*." His eyes widen, and I already see him ready to backtrack and call everything off. But I can't let him. I'll never find someone as perfect. I mean, he even rides a bike! So I edge another sheet of paper toward him. "And as per the final part of our agreement, these are all the brands we're shooting Super Bowl ads with, and that I could get you castings for."

Diego stares at me with an appalled look, followed by a questioning side glare of who-is-this-crazy-person-I'm-having-lunch-with? Then he lowers his eyes to the list, and his expression switches to mmm-these-brands-are-really-cool-and-how-many-people-watch-the-super-bowl-again?

I've just delivered an exemplary carrot-and-stick performance. He's in.

"I still think moving in together is too much," Diego says, a tad too loud.

The ladies to my left look up at us open-mouthed for a second, and then snicker between themselves. And even our server seems to have a satisfied little smirk on her face as she deposits our plates on the table. Wow, this man can really bring female rivalry to a whole new level.

"Maybe," I say, pointedly lowering my voice. "But I can't risk either of us slipping up in front of my family, not even on the smallest thing. And what are you complaining about? I'm offering you a free stay in Manhattan for two weeks."

Before he has time to come up with a thousand plausible reasons not to move in with the crazy cat lady, I push my point. "And anyway, I'm at work twelve to fourteen hours a day, so we wouldn't clash too much. And you'd be free to come and go as you like, with no more long commutes. From my apartment, you can get everywhere in Manhattan in fifteen minutes on the subway. You can go to your Santa gigs, or go to castings, or whatever it is you do all day." I still read doubt in his eyes, so I end with a cocksure, "It's non-negotiable."

I try to keep a straight face as panic rises in my throat. If he bails, I'm fried. I will have to confess my lies to my mom and suffer the greatest humiliation of my life.

He stares at me for a second, back at the brands list, and then sighs. "Ah, hell." He grabs his beer and takes a long sip. "In for a penny..."

The air leaves my lungs, and I relax for the first time since I got here. At least now I know I have a potential second career as a poker player.

We eat our lunch in silence. It's one of the most awkward meals I've ever had. All the more reason for him to move in—this is exactly the sort of thing we need to fix before the holidays.

When the bill arrives, I slip my credit card into the folder and sign the receipt once the server brings it back.

"How was your taco?" I ask Diego, trying to break the ice.

"Bit too fancy. I should've stuck with the classic."

"Aw, don't tell our server, she's going to be crushed."

Diego gives me a brief smile, and then the awkward silence is back.

After a few eternally long moments, he asks, "When do you want me to move in?"

"Tonight, if you can. The sooner the better." I grab my phone and text him the address. "That's me," I say.

"Whenever after 8 p.m. is fine."

"Great. Anything else?"

"Ah, yes." I fish a brown manila envelope out of my bag and slide it across the table toward him. "This is for you."

He looks skeptical again.

"What's this?"

"The first half of your payment," I reply, nonplussed.

Diego chuckles and shakes his head. "You brought an envelope full of cash?"

"Yeah, why? What did you expect?"

Still grinning, he says, "I don't know, PayPal?"

Oh. That would've made a lot of sense, actually. I guess I got a bit caught up in the movie stereotype. I blush and shrug, getting up. "I can do that if you prefer."

"Nah," Diego says, also standing. "Cash is fine." He makes the envelope disappear into an inside pocket of his jacket.

"Okay, then, see you tonight." I don't know if we should hug, or kiss on the cheek, or whatever... We'll need to decide what our thing is, but for now, I simply give him a professional nod and stroll out of the restaurant without looking back.

Five

Santa Claus Is Coming To Town

> Heading home now

A new text from Blair.

> Want to do something fun tonight?

Yeah, to get to know my fake boyfriend better.

So Blair will be home tonight. Good, as I need to catch her up on my crazy decisions of the past two days. And bad, as afterward, I need to convince her to traipse all the way back to Brooklyn on a cold December night.

> Great, almost there myself

> We need to talk

> Oh, okay

> Everything all right?

> Yeah

A CHRISTMAS DATE

> Just promise to keep an open mind

Now I'm curious

Hints?

> No can do

> You wouldn't believe it anyway

More radical than the hair?

> Definitely

Should I be worried?

> No

> Just open-minded

Wish I had my running shoes with me

This train is way too slow

See you at home

Blair is the only person I'm going to tell. A, because I can trust her, and B, because I have no choice if we're driving to Old Saybrook, our hometown, together. Our families live across the street from each other, so she'll need to corroborate my fake romance.

I get home first and set Blair's favorite herbal tea to steep. We're going to share a mug, and she'll come on board. Or maybe I should spike her mug with booze.

Five minutes later, just as the tea is ready, the key turns in the lock and Blair walks in.

"Gosh, it's freezing out there!" she says. "Oh, great, you made tea. Just what I need right now." She kicks off her heels, drapes her coat on the back of the couch, and takes a stool at the kitchen bar.

I fill two mugs from the other side of the bar and hand her one. She wraps her fingers around it to warm them and studies me. "So, my favorite tea, huh? What's going on?"

I'm ready to confess, when she continues, "But before you say anything, I spoke with Richard and we've decided we don't have to push the moving in together thing. Definitely something we'll think about in the new year. And I'm going to spend more nights home, I promise."

"Err, actually..." I take a sip of tea. "I kind of need you to do the opposite."

Blair's eyes widen. "What? Why?"

"I'm having a house guest and I need your room."

"Who?"

I plaster an innocent smile on my face. "This is the part where you keep an open mind…"

She narrows her eyes at me. "Nicola Addison Moore, what have you done?"

"I've hired someone."

"Like a housekeeper?"

"More like a fake boyfriend."

Blair chokes on the sip of tea she was drinking and sputters it all over the counter. She tries to ask questions but can only cough and spatter. I take advantage of her momentary inability to talk and say my piece. "And it might seem crazy, but I can't go home single and pathetic this year. Paul is going to spend the holidays at our place because he's *family* now, and I can't survive a whole week under the same roof with them by myself. My mom wanted to give them my room, my bed…"

Blair's face is still super red from the choking, and even if her eyes are still teary, I can tell she can speak now. Only she doesn't seem sure what she wants to say. She shakes her head, drops the mug on the bar, and starts massaging her temples. "Okay, let's pretend for a second I don't find this whole idea completely absurd, and that I'm keeping an open mind." She looks back up at me. "Who is this guy? Where did you find him? And you asked him to move in? In my room? Without even asking me?"

I lean back against the stove, keeping the bar between us in case she decides to throttle me. She's right, I should've at least asked her first, but I was desperate, and that's what I tell her. "I'm sorry, but I didn't know what else to do…"

"But why do you need to live together?"

"We have to fool my family for a whole week, and it needs to be a good act… so we need to appear comfortable around each other."

"But who is this person?"

"An actor. I hired him off the KCU's database."

"Have you worked with him before?"

"No."

"So you've invited a complete stranger to live with you?"

"Desperate times, desperate measures."

"But he could be a psycho, a rapist, a serial killer."

"I'm sure he's none of those things."

"Yeah? How sure?"

"You can tell for yourself. He'll be here in..." I check my watch. "Half an hour."

"WHAT?" Blair shoots up from her stool and starts pacing around, shaking her head. "He's coming over *tonight?* But where will he sleep?"

"The couch? I thought you were spending the night at Richard's."

"And what if I were? You would've let him sleep in my bed without even asking?"

"Oh, come on. We've always used each other's rooms to host friends and family when the other was away, *without* asking."

"Yeah, right. Friends and family, not complete strangers who—"

"Well, what was I supposed to do?" I raise my voice as tears of frustration fill my eyes. "Be the good girl, go home, and let Julia have everything she wants? Hasn't she taken enough from me? I won't let her win this time."

"Okay, let's calm down here." Blair's face softens. "The engagement and Paul joining your family for the holidays have been huge shocks. But is hiring this dude really the only answer?"

"If you have a better idea that will let me keep my sanity and my room back home, shoot…"

Blair goes to sit on the couch, and after a moment I join her. I can almost hear the wheels in her brain turning, trying to find an alternative solution. But after five minutes of scrunching her face and staring into space, she turns toward me, defeated.

"I've got nothing," she huffs.

"See? I'm not crazy."

"Apparently not. What do you need from me?"

"For you to get on board with the plan and pretend you've known Diego for a few months—"

"Diego?"

"Yeah, that's him."

"Surname?"

"O'Donnell."

She types both into her phone.

"What are you doing?"

"Saving his generalities in case you disappear and the police need them."

"Hey, you're the only person I know who ever got in trouble with the cops."

"I was a victim of the justice system, and we're not talking about me."

"I thought you were asking how you could be supportive."

Blair sighs. "I was. Anything else you need?"

I make big, Puss-in-Boots eyes at her. "Could you free some closet space in your room?"

***

When the doorbell rings, Blair is already packed and ready to go back to Brooklyn. She's called Richard, who'll come to pick her up in a bit—she's asked for enough time to make sure Diego is no Charlie Manson, I suspect.

"He's coming up," I announce after buzzing Diego in.

"Good." Blair has settled with her butt against the back of the couch and is staring at the door with the same rapt expression of a hawk scanning the woods for squirrels.

I wait by the threshold, keeping the door half open and feeling ridiculously nervous.

When I spot Diego walking down the hall, I have a moment's hesitation. With his leather jacket, dark looks, and biker helmet, he really is a "bad boy" personification. I just hope Blair can get past first impressions.

"Hi," I call. "I'm down here."

He sees me and waves, quickening his pace. "Hey, boss," he greets me, more easygoing than he's been in all our previous meetings.

Good, I need him to be relaxed to withstand Blair's sure-to-come interrogation.

"My roommate's here." I give him a heads up on the situation before letting him in. "She's waiting for her boyfriend to pick her up."

"Oh, okay. Do I have to act boyfriendly, then?"

A thrill spider walks down my spine, making me wonder what his "acting boyfriendly" would entail, but I shake the thought away as quickly as it popped into my head.

"No need," I say. "She knows."

I finally nudge the door open all the way and let him in.

"Diego, this is Blair. Blair, Diego."

My best friend does a good job of dropping her jaw only for a second before resuming her studiously scolding expression.

"Hi, I'm Diego."

He offers her a hand, and she shakes it.

"Blair."

"Nice to meet you," he says, then turns toward me, asking, "Is there somewhere I can drop these?"

I take the helmet from him and place it on the bar. "You can leave your bag in Blair's room. This way." I beckon him to follow me.

He drops the bag on her bed, and before he can do or say anything, she's giving him the rules.

"I freed this side of the closet for you," Blair says, opening the door to show him. "And the nightstand. Everything else is still filled with my things, so please don't touch anything."

"I'm not diseased, you know?" Diego frowns, more jokingly than serious.

"No, I don't. Because I know nothing about you. For all *I know,* you could be a serial killer."

"I sense some hostility," Diego says, again not serious.

"Well, sorry if I'm not super-duper pleased about my best friend's idea to invite a perfect stranger to live in the house with her."

"Hey, don't take it out on me." He lifts his hands in a surrender gesture. "I tried to convince her it wasn't necessary."

We all move back into the living room. Diego sits on a stool while Blair walks into the kitchen. I lean against the back of the couch and observe warily as Blair takes a glass out of a cabinet and cleans it with a rag—even though it's perfectly clean already. Then she disappears into the bathroom and comes back with one of those plastic bags you have to use for liquids on a plane. Still holding the glass enveloped in the rag, she hands it to Diego.

"Hold this, please."

He takes it from her, looking rather puzzled. As am I.

"Okay, now put it in here," Blair instructs, keeping the plastic bag open.

Diego drops the glass in the bag and, just as he's looking back up with a questioning expression, Blair snaps a photo with her phone.

"What the hell?" he asks, blinded by the flash.

"All right, Mister, just be advised that if something happens to my best friend, I have your name, your picture, and your fingerprints." She dangles the makeshift evidence bag in front of him. "The police will find you in no time."

Diego seems more amused than offended. "Paranoid much?"

"I'm sorry," I say. "She's just being overprotective."

"You bet I am," Blair snaps. "And you should also be aware that I have a trained attack dog who'd chew you to pieces if you so much as harm a hair on her head."

To describe Chevron as a trained attack dog would be like saying Diego is a Danny DeVito lookalike—oil and water.

"And now…" Blair reaches into her bag, which is sitting on the stool next to Diego, and takes out a business card and a pen. She scribbles something on the blank side and hands it to him.

"What's this?" he asks.

"My business card," Blair says, nonplussed. "There's an address written on the back. We're casting a New Year's fashion photo-shoot. The screening starts at 10.30 a.m. on Tuesday. Don't be late."

Diego smiles. "Do you always invite presumed serial killers to job interviews, or do you only need an extra mug shot?"

Blair's answer dies on her lips as the buzzer goes off, and the only thing I can think is, *"Saved by the bell!"*

My roomie gathers the suitcase she's prepared for her ten-day stay at Richard's, and I walk her to the door. We pause just outside the hall to say goodbye.

"Thank you," I tell her. "I know you don't like this."

"Just be careful," she whispers. "And lock yourself into your room tonight."

I roll my eyes.

"Promise," she insists.

"I promise."

"All right." Blair hugs me. "Call me if you need anything. I'll keep my phone on."

"I will, but I'm sure it won't be necessary."

We hug again, and then I watch her go until she disappears inside the elevator.

So! Time to enjoy my first cozy evening with my fake boyfriend.

Filled with trepidation, I push the door open and walk back into my apartment.

Six

The Twelve Days of Christmas

Inside, Diego is standing in the living room, looking around as if he's afraid to touch anything.

"So that went well," I say sarcastically, shutting the door behind me.

"Are all your friends that feisty?" he asks.

"Forgive Blair, it's my fault. I totally blindsided her with"—I wiggle a finger between us—"this. Told her you were moving in only an hour ago."

"Smooth."

"Well," I snap. "Buying a boyfriend wasn't on my Christmas shopping list until a few days ago." That came out too harsh. "Sorry, I didn't mean to be rude, it's just that this whole situation is stressful for me, too. Can we pretend my best friend just told you *mi casa es tu casa* and move on?"

"Sure."

"Great. This is a spare set of keys." I grab it from the cabinet in the hall and hand it to him. "So you can come and go as you like. The blue is for the main door downstairs, and the big one opens this door here. The others, you won't need."

"Got it." Diego stashes the keys away in his jeans pocket.

Gosh, this is super awkward. Well, what did I expect? I don't know this guy, we've got nothing in common, and the situation per se is less than relaxing.

"So," I say, trying to loosen up the atmosphere. "What

would you do if this was a regular night at home?"

"Probably play on the Xbox with my roommate."

"Sorry, no Xbox here, only that." I gesture to the small TV in the living room. "How about an old-fashioned chat?"

"Okay. You want to start scripting our relationship?"

"Nah, it's late, and I've no energy left. No creative juices flowing right now. Why don't we cover the basics for tonight? Where we're from, what our families are like, stuff like that."

"Yeah, great."

"You want a glass of wine?"

I need a drink. I'm definitely too nervous around this guy, and the feeling has to go quickly if my charade is to be believed by anyone.

"Yes, please." Diego nods and goes to settle on the couch.

"Red or white?"

"Whatever is fine."

I pick a bottle of red, grab two glasses, a corkscrew, and join him on the couch—sitting on the opposite, farthest end of it. I start maneuvering the corkscrew, damaging the cork more than I should in the process, when Diego says, "Here, let me."

I hand over the bottle and, in a couple of quick moves, Diego has the cork removed and undamaged. He pours two generous glasses.

"You're pretty handy with a bottle," I comment.

"Well, modeling and acting only pay for a small part of the bills. I'm a part-time server at a steakhouse downtown."

"When you're not busy being a Santa impersonator."

"Hey, I need all the money I can get. Wouldn't be here otherwise."

Yeah, right. We might need to get comfortable with each other, but I have to remember this is still an employer-employee kind of relationship.

"Is it going to be a problem for the restaurant—you not showing for a whole week over Christmas break?"

"Nah. I only work there three nights a week, and I've asked my roommate to cover for me. Screech could use the extra money, too, and the owner doesn't care as long as someone shows up to do the job."

"You guys call each other weird names. He called you 'Dunk' over the phone."

"Those are our gaming avatars."

"Oh, cool. Anyway, I'm glad I didn't mess with your work schedule."

"On the contrary." He flips Blair's business card between his fingers. "Is your friend's magazine legit?"

"Pretty new, but legit. Just a few months ago they did a fashion shoot with Saskia Landon."

Diego low whistles. "Then I'd better stay on your friend's good side."

"Blair is very friendly, usually. Earlier, she was just being overprotective. It's nothing personal."

"So, you two have been friends long?"

"Forever." I sip the wine, and its warm taste helps me ease into the conversation. "We grew up across the street from each other in Old Saybrook, a tiny coastal town a hundred miles north of here."

"Never heard of it."

"Small town." I shrug and take another sip of wine. "You from around here, too?"

"No, I'm originally from Chicago. My family still lives there."

"Is your family big?"

"Yep. I have three brothers, one older and two younger. And too many uncles, aunts, and cousins on both my dad and my mom's side to count. I guess that's what happens when an Irish man marries an Italian woman."

Oh, so that explains his uncommon name, the Mediterranean colorings of his skin and hair, and the fact that he speaks Italian paired with the Irish surname, green eyes, and freckles.

"What do your brothers do?"

"Johnathan, the older, is a cop, just been promoted to detective. Greg, the other middle child, is a fireman. And the baby, Adam, is a cop, too, but he's trying out for the FBI next year."

"Whoa, sounds like a committed public-service bunch."

"Well, my dad's been a cop for forty years..." He grimaces. "I'm the only one not to have followed in his footsteps, more or less."

"Do they give you a hard time about it?"

"Used to. I can't even remember how many sermons I had to hear about how acting wasn't a sound career choice. Now, I think they just feel sorry for me." Diego looks away in the distance. "My dream was easier to sell ten years ago. But after so many years without a breakthrough, they must wonder what I'm still doing in this city working as a server, and what my plan is."

"So, you're a member of the sibling-to-be-pitied club, huh?"

He frowns. "Why? Your parents aren't happy with your career?"

"Unfortunately, it has more to do with the lack of a diamond ring on my finger at the late age of thirty, and my inability to supply chubby grandkids."

"Oooooh, I know the drill," Diego sympathizes. "Two of my brothers are already married, and both have kids."

"Wow, you weren't kidding when you said you had a big family."

"Nope."

"You'll have to write me a family tree so I can learn their names."

"Why? It's not like you'll ever meet them."

"No, but my mom or sister could ask questions." Knowing them, they certainly will. "It'd be weird if I knew nothing about your family, at least the basics." I grab a pad and a pencil from the coffee table and hand them to him. "Just put down your mom, dad, brothers, and their spouses and kids' names."

Diego sets his almost-empty wine glass on the table and takes the notepad.

"Refill?" I ask, as he writes down the O'Donnell genealogy.

"Yes, please."

I top up his glass and wait for him to be done before asking my next question. "Why New York? Wouldn't LA have been the more obvious choice for an aspiring actor?"

Diego sighs. "Call me a romantic, but my heart is in the theater. Nothing can top performing in front of a live audience. The adrenaline of walking onto a stage, knowing you have to deliver every single time, and that if you make a mistake, there won't be a second take. It's priceless."

"So, what's your favorite show?"

"Ever, or recently?"

"Let's keep it recent."

"Then *Harry Potter and the Cursed Child.*"

"Oh, I read the book—script, whatever—but it was a bit of a letdown."

"Of course, because it wasn't supposed to be experienced that way. You need to buy a ticket and go see the actual show. It'll blow your mind, I promise."

"Really? I don't know... I grew up reading Harry Potter... Do you remember the excitement when a new book was about to come out, and the desperation when you finished it and knew there'd be at least another two years to wait before the next one?"

"Yeah, it was the best and the worst."

"It's my favorite series ever, and I've read it so many times I think I've consumed the books beyond repair... so when *The Cursed Child* came out I was over the moon, but then I read it and... meh!"

Diego nods understandingly. "Nothing will ever top a new Harry Potter book, I agree. But if you approach *The Cursed Child* as a play and not a book, it's so much better. You won't regret watching it."

I smile. "Okay, maybe I'll try it..."

Diego's enthusiasm when he speaks about Broadway is contagious. This guy is turning out like nothing I would've expected from just looking at his picture. I thought he was going to be one of those vain, self-absorbed male models who pay more attention to their skin products than I do. But he's no egomaniac.

"What about you?" Diego asks. "Have you always wanted to work at an advertising agency?"

"I studied marketing and visual design in college, but I ended up in my line of work more by chance. I met my former boss at a recruiting event, and he gave an inspiring speech on what they did at KCU, on how they fostered new talent, and how a college graduate would thrive at their agency. So, I guess I chose a mentor more than a profession. And it worked out pretty well. I love what I do and the people I do it with, so…"

Diego grins. "Now you're only missing that diamond ring on your finger, and to pop out the standard two point five chubby babies before you turn forty."

I laugh. "Nailed it."

I'm not sure if it's the wine or the fact that we've been talking for a while, but I'm getting more relaxed around him. Same as if there was a regular person on the couch next to me, instead of an impossibly sexy hunk from another planet.

We chat a little more and finish the wine before I realize how late it is.

"Sorry," I say, getting up. My head is dizzier than I'd like. "I have an early morning tomorrow. You?"

"I switched my shifts at the restaurant to lunch, so I'll be free in the evenings."

"Perfect. Well, you have your keys, and the Wi-Fi password is on the back of the box." I point at the modem sitting next to the TV. "The fridge is stocked if you want to eat something; just beware of Blair's vegetarian crap."

"I will." Diego smiles and gets up. And I watch, astonished, as he gathers both our glasses and the bottle and rinses the former in the sink after throwing the latter in the recycle bin. Good looking, down to earth, *and* with perfect manners. *Impressive!*

"Mind if I use the bathroom first?" I ask.

He shrugs. "It's your house."

Feeling again awkward, I wave. "Good night, then."

"Night."

When I come out of the bathroom, Diego is in Blair's room, out of sight. I slip into my room, change into my PJs and, feeling a bit silly, I lock the door.

***

The next morning, my phone starts ringing the moment I resurface above ground from the subway station closest to work.

I lodge my earbuds in place and pick up.

"Are you alive?" Blair demands, as I begin the short walk to my office building. "Where are you?"

"I answered the phone; that should be a good indication I'm still breathing," I say, stopping at a red traffic light and wrapping the collar of my coat tighter around my neck. "I'm walking to the office. You?"

"Me, too. Sorry, I've just been so worried all night."

The light turns green and I cross the street. "No need to be; Diego is a perfectly nice guy."

"Nice or not, Richard agrees with me: you were reckless to invite a total stranger into our house."

"You told him?" I almost stop in the middle of the road, but the Manhattan pedestrian crowd prompts me forward.

"Of course I did. How else was I supposed to explain my late night pick up request?"

"Saying you wanted to spend time with him?"

"Oh, please, I'd just left him, he would've known something was up. He also said he wants to meet this guy before we drive home with him."

"Oh my gosh," I sigh, exasperated, as I open the door of my favorite Starbucks. "Richard is just as paranoid as you are."

"No, we're both responsible adults."

"Hold on a second..." I say, then mouth, "The usual," to the barista, switch my phone to the Starbucks app to pay, and go wait in line for my order. "Okay, Mr. and Mrs. Responsible Adults, you can both relax..."

"Yeah, why?"

"Diego's entire family is in law enforcement. He's hardly serial killer material."

"Mmm, hello? Have you seen *Dexter?*"

"Dexter only zapped the bad guys, so I should be safe anyway, no?"

"Unless one of his serial killer buddies decides to take it out on the girlfriend."

"*Fake* girlfriend, and, Blair, life isn't a TV show. But if Richard really wants to meet Diego, tell your boyfriend to come to the casting on Tuesday. But please also tell him to be subtle and not to interrogate Diego, deal?"

"Oh, great, I wasn't sure he'd come."

"Why? Because you took his fingerprints? It's a good opportunity for him. He's a professional; why wouldn't he come?"

"I don't know... He could be busy planning his next murder?"

"I'm hanging up."

"No, nooo. I was just kidding. So, how did your first night go? What did you guys do?"

"Skinny mocha vanilla latte for Nikki," a barista shouts.

I shove the phone back into my coat pocket and grab the coffee, gladly wrapping my hands around the warm paper cup, before returning to the freezing temperatures of a New York morning in December.

"We opened a bottle of wine and chatted, you know, to cover the basics: family, education, career..."

"And how was it?"

"Pretty cozy; he's an easy guy to talk to. I mean, for someone that looks so, mmm…"

Blair supplies the definition for me, "Freaking hot?"

"Yeah."

"You're not getting *too* cozy, are you? He's there only because you're paying him."

"I'm aware, thank you. I was just saying that I expected a narcissistic showoff, and instead, he's rather easy going, funny, even… But don't worry, he's not my type at all."

"Yeah, about that… I was wondering why you picked someone so… *not you.* Isn't your family going to get suspicious?"

I stop a few steps away from my building's main entrance. "You want the ugly truth? The one I could tell only my best friend without being judged?"

"Yeah-ah…"

"He's Julia's type," I confess. "For once, I want her to be jealous of me, even if it's just for a second and it's all fake. Am I too pathetic?"

"No, you're not, and I don't have any siblings to compete with, so I'm really not an expert on the subject of sisterly envy. I can't even begin to think what I'd do if my imaginary sister was marrying Richard, so…"

"Thank you," I say, relieved she's in my corner no matter what crazy ideas get into my head. "Listen, I'm at the office, I gotta go."

"Yeah, I'm almost there, too. Okay, I'll talk to you soon, and please send regular texts to let me know you're alive."

I roll my eyes but smile. "I will."

***

I haven't been seated at my desk five minutes before my cell phone goes off again. It's Julia. Ugh, majorly not in the mood for another wedding planning rant. I let the call go unanswered. Three seconds later, my internal line rings, signaling Melanie is calling me.

"Yeah?" I say.

"I have your sister on line two."

I could tell Melanie to make an excuse for me—that I'm in a meeting, or not at the office—but I know Julia. If she's decided we have to talk now, she'll just pester me until I surrender and answer. Compared to my sister, my mom is a restrained serial caller.

I sigh. "All right, put the call through." Melanie hangs up. I wait for the external line's button to flash and push it. "Hello?"

"Mom says I can't have your room."

"Good morning to you, too," I reply. "And, yes, Mom would be correct."

"But Nikki, I'm bringing my fiancé home for the holidays. We can't stay in my room. Yours is bigger."

"Our rooms are exactly the same."

"Okay, but I can't make Paul sleep in my castle princess bed."

"I'm sorry about that, but when given the chance to choose a bed, you should've picked something more practical."

"I was eight."

"And I was ten. Didn't stop me from ordering a perfectly sensible queen bed."

Truth is, my only guiding principle at the time was to do the exact opposite of what Julia did. So, when she opted for a fairy tale bunk bed—pink, complete with turrets,

64

crenellations, and tulle drapes—I went for the most serious, adult-looking bed I found at the shop.

"But Paul won't fit…"

"Then ask Mom to get rid of the princess bed and buy a replacement."

"But I love that bed."

"Well, sorry… You'll have to pick: either Paul sleeps in the princess bed, or the bed goes."

I take a little smudge of satisfaction in knowing Julia is not going to have exactly everything she wants.

"But why can't you switch?"

"Because my boyfriend won't fit in the princess bed any better."

"Oh, so you really have a boyfriend?"

"Yeah," I say.

"Since when? I thought Mom misunderstood."

Sure, because it would be so impossible for me to have a boyfriend. No matter that it sort of is impossible. The fact that Julia would just assume… Grrrrrrr. I bite the receiver before I continue.

"A few months."

"Why didn't you tell me? Who is this guy?"

"Jules, I'm just more private with my life than you, and right now I'm at the office, *working*. I don't have time to gossip."

"Work, work, work. You always have to work. I've been trying your private phone for an hour this morning, and it was always busy."

"I was talking to someone else."

"Who, your boyfriend?"

"No, Blair."

"Oh, the sister you wish you'd had."

I stare at the ceiling, trying to keep calm. It's definitely too early for one of Julia's dramatic scenes. "Why are you throwing a tantrum?" I ask.

"Because you're dating someone and didn't even think of telling me. I had to learn it from Mom!" she whines. "How long has Blair known him? It's like I don't exist for you."

Julia and I have never been close, and since she's been dating Paul, the distance has increased. I love her, she's my sister, and if she needed a kidney I'd give it to her without a moment's hesitation. But we're so different, and with her dating the guy I love... It's just hard.

"I'm sorry, Jules, but until recently I wasn't sure the relationship was that serious, or even worth mentioning."

"But why didn't you tell me the other day?"

"That was your moment, your big announcement... I didn't want to steal your thunder."

"Really?"

"Really."

"So who is this guy? When am I going to meet him?"

"At Christmas like the rest of the family."

"Why? We're both in the city; can't we meet up earlier?"

"I'm sorry, but no. I'm super busy until the agency closes, and Diego is super busy, too."

"Diego... Mmm, cool name. What does he look like?"

"Julia." I use my best older sister tone. "I don't have time to chat, but I'm sure you're going to like him." *Maybe a bit too much,* an evil little voice adds inside my head. "I really have to go now."

"You're a buzz kill."

"Love you, too. Bye." I hang up and lean back in my chair, massaging my temples.

Another twelve days to C-Day and I'm already about to explode. I just hope this mastermind plan of mine won't epically backfire on me.

Seven

Baby, It's Cold Outside

When I get home that evening, the house smells like... mmm... my mom's kitchen. For a second I panic, thinking she couldn't resist meeting my boyfriend and decided to drop by unannounced. But I let out a breath of relief as soon as I step out of the hallway and see there's only Diego seated at the kitchen bar, eating dinner.

"Hey," I say. "What smells good? Did you make dinner?"

"No, the chef at the restaurant always feeds me scraps. Sorry I didn't wait for you, but I was starving."

"Don't worry, I usually don't get home this late. What are you having?"

"Homemade lasagna, best in New York. There's plenty left, and it's still warm. Marisa always gives me way too much. Want some?"

My dinner plan was to order something from the Thai restaurant down the street, which is what I usually do when Blair isn't home to prepare a healthy dinner for the both of us. But homemade lasagna beats that a hundred to one.

"Sure there's enough for two?" I ask.

"Yeah, even three or four."

"All right, then."

I grab a plate, a glass, and a fork from the cabinets and sit at the kitchen bar next to him.

Diego scoops me a generous helping of lasagna out of the aluminum tray. "Here's the best lasagna you'll ever have—unless you meet my mom. No one beats my mom's."

I take a bite and… "Mmm… this is delicious." The lasagna is both creamy and rich, but not overwhelming. I could devour a whole tray of this.

"Told ya." Diego smiles. "So, how was your day?"

"Stupid, yours?"

"A regular shift at the restaurant, nothing exciting," he says, then smirks. "What happens on a stupid day?"

"Your boss poaches an unhappy client from another agency, and delivers the pitch but only brings the creative team with him…"

Diego finishes up his plate and rounds the bar to rinse his dish and drop it in the dishwasher. Gosh, he really is tidy. I would've dropped the dirty dish in the sink and maybe splashed water on it. I tend to postpone house chores until they become overwhelmingly necessary.

"So." Diego leans against the counter as I scarf down the last bites of lasagna. "Did the creatives drop the ball?"

"Oh, no, they wowed the client."

"And that's bad because?"

"Every creative pitch has to be vetted by a producer because we're the reality check. We understand what can be done in how much time, and at what budget… You leave the creatives free, and they'll go overboard."

"And they did this time?"

"For sure. The ad they pitched is brilliant and witty, but it's a production nightmare." I finish the lasagna and lick the fork before dropping it on the empty plate. "Too many actors, too many locations, and too little time. Not to talk about the budget; we'll be lucky if we break even on this one."

Promptly, Diego scoops up the plate, rinses it, and drops

it into the dishwasher. "Where do you keep the dish soap?"

"There're pods under the sink."

He loads one, studies the dishwasher's buttons for a few seconds, pushes a couple, and the machine awakens.

"Your boss must really trust you if he put you on this assignment," Diego says, coming back to my side of the counter.

I stand up and move to the couch, where I kick off my shoes. "You have a future in management, you know?"

Diego joins me on the sofa, sticking to "his" end. "Yeah, why?"

"That's exactly what my boss told me to sell me the project, '…You're the only one who can pull it off… Can't trust anyone else… Blah, blah, blah…'"

Diego smirks. "Then it must be true."

"True or not, the bottom line stays the same: I'm screwed. There's even a cat in the ad. I mean, *a cat.*"

"You don't like cats?"

"I love cats. I'm one hundred percent a cat person. But on set, they're a nightmare. Trained animals are expensive, and a scene to turn out decent needs a million takes, meaning long hours and money and time I don't have. What about you, cats or dogs?"

Please say cats, please say cats…

"Cats…"

Yay! I do a mental victory dance. "How come? Guys usually go for dogs."

"Blame my mom; we've never had less than three cats in the house. And she keeps feeding all the neighborhood cats as well, stray or not. So I guess I was groomed into being a cat person."

"Great, I can't stand dogs."

"Why?"

"They lick, they're smelly… Ew, gross."

"Doesn't your roommate have a dog?"

"Chevron? She's different. She's a cat's soul trapped in a dog's body, know what I mean?"

Diego chuckles. "Not really."

"You'll see when you meet her."

He shakes his head, amused.

"What?" I ask self-consciously.

"You make little sense sometimes."

"Why?"

"A cat person who claims to hate dogs usually doesn't own one."

"Correction, my roommate has a dog. I've begged her to get a cat from the day we moved in together, but she always said the apartment was too small to have a pet. Then she found a stray puppy and suddenly we had enough room for a sixty-pound dog. So, really, it's her not making sense."

Diego nods. "Agreed."

"Hey, you want something to drink? Sorry I didn't offer. We have wine, beer…"

"Are you drinking?"

"No, my brain gets too scrambled if I drink two nights in a row, and I need to be on top of my game this week."

"Tomorrow's the weekend."

"Well, yeah, but thanks to my new assignment I have to drop by the office. You have your Santa thing tomorrow, right?"

"Yeah, the afternoon shift from two to six."

"That's perfect. We can go Christmas shopping together in the morning, work after lunch, and meet up again for dinner later. Sound good?"

"Christmas shopping?"

"Yeah, we need to buy each other presents. My family is big on present unwrapping on the twenty-fifth."

"Oh." He frowns.

"Don't worry, I'm buying my present. We just have to think of something smart, and unique, and romantic..."

Diego looks like he's just swallowed lemons. "Fine, but I should warn you: I hate Christmas shopping."

I laugh. "That makes two of us, but we gotta do what we gotta do... Anything on your letter to Santa?"

"Nothing you can put under wrapping paper..." he says, with that Broadway spark in his eyes.

"Know the feeling," I agree. My biggest Christmas wish has nothing to do with material things, either. And anyway, we're all supposed to be good at Christmas, so I can't really wish for my sister's life to crumble to pieces... But I could wish to feel less freaking alone all the time, or to forget Paul, or to fall in love with someone who loves me back for a change... Yeah, those would all be much better wishes...

"Are you okay?" Diego asks.

"Yeah, why?"

"You sort of went all glassy-eyed."

"Sorry." I massage my temples. "I'm just exhausted. What do you say we call it a night so we can start early on the shopping tomorrow morning?

Diego grimaces. "Ho ho ho," he chants in a deep voice nothing like his own.

"I never understood how you actors do that."

"Do what?"

"Change your voice on command."

"It's all diaphragm, throat, and nose work." With every word he changes his voice—throaty, nasal, husky—making me laugh. "And many hours of practice."

"That's amazing."

"All right, boss," he says, back to his normal tone. He gets up and offers me a hand. "Let's go to bed."

I take his hand and he lifts me up, and for a second we end up standing really close to each other. So close I can smell his clean soap scent... simple, but intoxicating. And I haven't had sex in too long to stand this close to the sexiest man I've ever met. And even if I don't like him that way, well... I'm still made of flesh...

"Okay, then," I say, sounding like an awkward teenager and trying hard not to blush. "Good night."

I move past him and go hide in my room. I barely hear his soft, "Night," reply before I shut the door and lock myself in.

***

I blink my eyes open to the sound of a blow dryer running.

What time is it?

A quick peek at my watch tells me it's already ten. So much for an early start. Sometimes I wish I could be one of those early risers, people who wake up at five a.m. on autopilot to go for a run. Someone like Blair. My roommate is so healthily annoying. But put me in a cozy bed and I could sleep in until noon every day. I don't know why I didn't set an alarm last night. Easy, because my phone has a weekly alarm programmed to let me sleep on the weekends.

I throw away the covers, get up, and swap PJs for a pair of sweatpants and a T-shirt. In front of the wardrobe mirror, I try to flatten my hair, preventing it from sticking out in all directions. I so wish it was still long enough to pull up in a bun. I miss buns.

Bun-less and still crazy-haired, I venture into the hall and almost collide with a semi-naked Diego. He's wearing only a towel around his hips, presenting me with the kind of naked chest usually reserved for steamy romance book covers. I try not to look, but my gaze gets drawn to the inviting V of muscle disappearing just below the towel, and I involuntarily bite my lower lip. I mentally slap myself, and my eyes snap back up to his face. His hair, fresh from the blow dry, is wilder than mine and gives him a tousled look that's hard to resist.

"Hi," I say.

"Morning."

"You been up long?"

"A couple of hours…"

"Why didn't you wake me?"

"I know you wanted an early start, but it didn't feel right to barge into your room to wake you, so I worked out a little instead."

A glorious image of him doing pushups and crunches bare chested is now permanently ingrained in my brain. And of course he'd be the kind of person who wakes up early on a Saturday to work out. A body like that just doesn't sculpt itself. I think of my soft belly and take back everything I just thought. Early risers are horrible people whose mission in life is to make us late sleepers feel guilty about our love for cushy pillows and snuggles under the comforter.

"No, you're right," I say. "I should've set an alarm… What do you say we go out for breakfast?" I stare at my watch. "It's too late to go shopping now, anyway. We can eat something and lay down the basis of our fake relationship instead."

"Yeah, I'm starving."

"Great, just give me time for a quick shower. Meet here in thirty?"

He winks at me. "All right, boss."

My stomach responds with a weird little flip. Maybe it wasn't the wink. Right, I'm probably just hungry.

We switch ends in the narrow hall, and I do my best to stick to the wall and not give in to the temptation to brush against all that bared muscle. Obstacle surpassed, I dive into the bathroom and hop into the shower.

One perk of short hair is that it takes less time to dry. So, in just under thirty minutes I'm all set and ready to go grab a coffee. Clad in black trousers and a gray knit sweater, casual-wear appropriate for the office, I go meet Diego down the hall and stop dead in my tracks again. Dressed Diego is no less heart-stopping than half-naked Diego. He's wearing a pair of light-faded jeans that fit his rear side so well they should be made illegal. And his biker jacket does nothing to tone down the sexiness. My mouth goes a little dry—too much sex appeal to handle on an empty stomach and without an ounce of caffeine in my system. I need breakfast.

We opt for the Starbucks around the corner. I order my usual skinny mocha vanilla latte and note that he goes for black coffee, super manly. As for food, we both get glazed donuts. At least he's not also one of those protein bars, healthy-eater types. I mean, nothing wrong with keeping a healthy diet and exercise routine, but I can't stand extremists. Julia sort of is a food extremist, but of course, I still love her. She's my sister; I have to.

"You always get black coffee?" I ask, as we sit at a table by the window.

"No, sometimes I venture into the wild lands of cappuccinos. Why?"

"Just trying to learn your habits. We should know these things about each other since we're"—I make air quotes—"dating. Skinny mocha vanilla lattes are my poison, and I prefer Starbucks."

"So you order fat-free milk, but a side of glazed, fried pastry is okay?"

I shrug. "Coffee tastes as good without the fatty milk and sugary syrup. Can't say the same about donuts." And to show my appreciation, I take a huge bite.

Diego smiles. "Duly noted." He rolls his coffee cup between his hands a few times, turning pensive.

"What?" I prompt him.

"Can I ask you one last time why you're doing this?"

"I already told—"

"Yeah, you need a date for the holidays. But... can I be honest?"

"Sure."

"Before getting to know you, I thought you had to have a major issue that scared men away or something, but spending the last few days together, you don't seem that..."

"Crazy?" I supply. "Well, thanks," I say, irritated.

"Don't get me wrong, I'm not trying to insult you. I only want to understand why a woman like you needs to hire someone to be her date."

My nostrils flare. "And by 'a woman like me' you mean?"

"Beautiful, smart, with a successful career, and with no clear social awkwardness... You shouldn't have any problems finding a man the traditional way."

That mollifies me a little... Did he really call me

beautiful? I stop myself from asking for confirmation and answer his question instead. "The problem isn't that I *can't* find a boyfriend *ever*. It's that I'm single *right now* while my baby sister just got engaged, and that's going to point an even bigger bullseye on the lack of that diamond ring on my finger. And this year, I can't bear it." I leave out the why. "Also, I don't want to be in a relationship for the sake of dating, and my job makes it hard to put in the time to find that special person."

And being in love with my sister's fiancé doesn't help, I add in my head.

"So you prefer to hire your dates off a catalog." Diego tries to keep a straight face, but the corners of his mouth twitch.

"Now you're just making fun of me."

He finally lets the smile take over his mouth, and gosh if he isn't a sight to behold when he smiles like that. "Sorry. I thought my mom was scary with her constant nagging about me needing to settle down, but you make your family sound so much worse…"

"They are, believe me, and that's why we need to be prepared if we want to fool them."

"Okay, so what's the story?"

"Let's start easy. Our first date, how did it happen?"

"We met in a bar?"

"Nah, too prosaic. We should stick to reality as much as we can, like they teach in spy movies."

"What's your angle here? We can't say you picked me off a catalog."

My time to smirk. "Actually, we sort of can…"

"How?"

"You came to the agency for a casting, and that's where

we met."

"And how did we move from the casting to the dating?"

"Ah, and the plot thickens... Any ideas?"

He frowns, concentrating. "You called me to say I had the job, and I told you I'd rather have a date."

"That sounds farfetched."

"Why?"

"Would you really have asked someone like me on a date?"

"And by 'someone like you,' you mean?"

"Someone who wouldn't look at home in a bikini catalog," I reply honestly.

He grimaces. "Ah, yes. Because we models can only date other models..."

"No, but..."

"But?"

"You're good looking, you know?"

Diego nods, serious, not one bit mollified.

"Above-average good looking..." I insist.

He nods again.

"So, it'd make sense you'd want to date someone as gorgeous as you."

"Why?"

"Because you can. Because why not?"

"Maybe because before I jump into bed with someone, I need a bit more of a connection. I'm not a horny teenager," he says harshly.

"Sorry, did I offend you?"

"Not really, I have thick skin. But don't assume I decide who to sleep with based only on how they look. Last time I slept with a woman only because she had a big rack, I was eighteen and in high school. So, when was the last time you slept with someone only because they had a nice ass?"

Totally against my will, an image of his perfectly round buns wrapped in white boxer briefs slips before my eyes. Those are buttocks that could definitely make me skip the need for an emotional connection.

I swallow, hoping I'm not blushing too hard. "I haven't... I mean... not really." At my visible embarrassment, his features soften a little. "Okay," I concede. "You've made your point. I won't make superficial assumptions about you from now on. Sorry."

He finally smiles. "Apology accepted, boss."

I try to bring the conversation back to its original track. "So, you asked me on a date. Why?"

"What do you mean, why?"

"What made you give up a job for me? If we tell that story, either my mom or my sister is going to ask why you were instantly smitten with me."

"Why? They can't accept a man could just ask you out?"

"We're women, we need details."

"Okay, I'll have an answer for when they ask."

"Can't you share it with me first?"

"No," he says, smirking. "It isn't ready yet."

I scowl at him.

"Don't worry." Diego leans forward in his chair. "I'll come up with something cheesy enough to sate your mom and sister's romance cravings."

I stare at him, unconvinced.

"Hey, I'm good at this stuff, I swear." He makes the Boy Scout salute.

I sure hope he is, with what I'm paying him. And if it turns out he sucks, I hope Mom and Julia will be too distracted by how good he looks to notice.

"Okay," I say. "I'm going to trust you on this. Oh, one last detail: What was the ad for?"

"Deodorant," Diego says without hesitation.

"Deodorant?"

"Yeah, what's wrong with it?"

"It isn't very romantic."

"We can say perfume or chocolate if you prefer, but deodorant makes it sound less staged, more real."

He has a point. "Deodorant it is."

An email flashes on my phone screen, and I get a peek of the time as well. "Wow, it's super late. Don't you have to be at the mall in like twenty minutes?"

He stares at his watch. "You're right."

We both get up, don our jackets, and exit the coffee shop in a hurry. It doesn't take long to be back at my building, where we stop outside to say goodbye.

"The subway is that way," I say. "I hope I haven't made you too late?"

"Nah, don't worry," Diego says, "it's only a ten-minute ride on the bike." He unlocks the saddle to take out his helmet. Then, as if on second thought, he adds, "Hey, you want a ride? Your office is on the way."

"No, no, you're already late, I don't want to make it worse."

"And you won't; we have all the time we need."

"I don't have a helmet," I protest.

"And I always carry a spare one." He opens a sort of detachable trunk and offers me a black helmet matching his.

"Err…"

When he sees me still hesitating, he asks, "You're not afraid of bikes, are you?"

"I wouldn't know," I say. "I've never been on one."

"Come on." Diego smiles encouragingly. "No girlfriend of mine, fake or otherwise, could skip a ride on my bike."

I quickly censor all the inappropriate scenarios my degenerate brain conjured up at the "take a ride on my bike" comment, and bravely nod, taking the helmet.

Eight

Sleigh Ride

The moment I climb on the bike behind Diego, I know I've made a mistake. This black monster is way too wobbly and unstable for my tastes.

At first, I try to keep my palms respectfully flat against Diego's sides while he backs the bike up. But the second he twists the accelerator, I wrap my arms around his waist as tightly as I can, my gloved fingers gripping his leather jacket for dear life. Especially when the bike stumbles off the curb with a roar of the engine, tires skidding on the road. The rumble is deafening; it vibrates up my legs to reach deep into my guts. I close my eyes, glue my head— helmet and all—to his broad back, and hope this ride will really only take ten minutes.

Diego works the clutches, making the bike gather speed, and I can't help but grip tighter as a little scream escapes my lips. Diego's chest starts to shake under my arms, and I have a strong suspicion he's laughing at me and my fear.

I couldn't care less. Right now, I'm focused on surviving the ride and getting off this death trap as soon as possible. Honestly, I don't understand how other women can find this sexy. Okay, I get the intimacy—physical, for how close the bodies touch, and emotional, for the trust one has to put in the driver to give away all control. And some women might like not being in control, or find the drop in their stomach at every acceleration thrilling, but I'm not one of them.

For the whole journey, I'm so pumped up with

adrenaline I don't notice the chill. I'm sure riding a bike in December should feel colder than this, but right now my universe is made only of Diego's body and how hard I can cling to him. My chest is pressed so close to his back we might've been fused.

Every turn, incline, and acceleration makes my heart pound faster. If this is what flying feels like, I'm glad humans were born without wings.

When we finally stop, I still hold onto him and keep my eyelids closed. It could be only a traffic light, and if I open my eyes now, I'm not sure I'll be able to handle the rest of the ride.

"Boss." Diego tries to turn back to look at me, but I'm holding on too tight. "We're here."

I'm still too scared to move.

"Nikki?" Diego calls again. "You can let go now."

Slowly, I release my koala grip on him and get off. I unhook my helmet and hand it to him, saying, "Let's never do this again."

"Don't say never, boss." Diego grins at me from underneath the helmet. I can tell he's smiling from the crinkles around his eyes. "It might grow on you…"

And with that he winks at me, pushes down on a pedal to revive the engine, opens the clutches, and disappears among the Manhattan traffic, leaving me standing on the curb in front of my building with legs still shaky from the sheer effort of pressing my thighs against his.

***

"I should buy you something for the bike," I say.

It's Sunday morning, and Diego and I are braving the holiday crowds to complete our Christmas shopping. I've already settled Julia with the fanciest wedding planner I could find in the mall's bookstore, Mom with a new recipe book, and Dad with the latest Ken Follett bestseller. Not the most original or thought-out presents, I'm aware, but I despise gift shopping.

I may or may not have also bought a novel for Paul a while ago. At the time, I wasn't even sure if I'd ever give it to him. But if he's going to spend the holidays at our house... I sort of have to. And, I mean, it's not like a thriller book—hardcover, special edition, signed by his favorite author—will send the message, *"I'm in love with you. Dump my sister and marry me instead."* Right?

"You need any new accessories?" I continue. "Gloves?" I couldn't help but notice his are a little worn out.

"Biker gear is expensive." Diego shrugs. "Why not get me a book like everybody else?"

"No, you're my *boyfriend.* I need to buy you something different, something special. You know a good biker gear shop?"

"There's one closer to your apartment; we can stop there on the way home."

"All right."

"We can go after buying my present for you. Have you decided what I'm getting you yet?"

I chew my lower lip. "I don't know."

Diego raises his brows. "A woman who can't choose her present. Impossible!"

"The best thing would be to get me a book. Or a cat. But I can't do the cat until Blair moves out, and it needs to be something showier than a book to impress my family."

"Remember, I'm a struggling artist." Diego grins.

"That's why we have to find a nice, thoughtful, but

inexpensive gift." I stare at the shopping windows surrounding us, kind of lost. "See the problem now?"

Just as the words leave my lips, we pass in front of a jewelry shop, and I'm captivated by a glass cube showcasing three rings, identical but for the color: one in silver, one in gold, and the last one in rose gold. The design is simple: plain gold bands, but... *with ears!*

"See something you like?" Diego asks.

I smile, pushing the shop's door open. "How about a cat ring?"

A girl in a bright-red suit hurries up to us, making me wonder if she's wearing a special holiday suit or if they go 'round all year long wearing that almost blinding shade of red.

"Hello, how may I help you today?" She has a chirpy, honey-like voice, which fits the festive-bonanza décor of the shop perfectly.

"We're here to buy a ring," I say.

"A ring, how wonderful." She twinkles at me. "Christmas present?" Her big, it's-that-time-of-the-year, sparkly eyes set on Diego next.

Err... She thinks we're a real couple Christmas shopping. Well, why wouldn't she?

I glance at Diego for help—but he's staring around the shop, completely unaware. And there's no way I'm launching into the whole story of how Diego is only a for-hire boyfriend in front of a bunch of strangers—there are three shop assistants in total, all in eye-sore red.

"Yeah." I smile awkwardly. "It's a gift, I mean, sort of—"

"That's wonderful! I'm Evelyn, and I'll be happy to assist you today," Evelyn chirps. "Did you already have something specific in mind?"

"Yes," I say. "The cat rings by the windows."

"Oh." Another one of the girls in red sighs. "They're so cute, aren't they?"

"Goodness." Evelyn takes my arm, steering me toward the showcase window, and leans in, lowering her voice to speak in a girl-to-girl tone. "The girls and I have a little contest every holiday season to find the cutest couple, and you've just knocked all competition out of the park! He's quite the catch. Lucky you!"

I should be proud of the admiration Diego is inspiring. After all, I've hired him to make sure my whole family shuts the hell up about my singlehood for one Christmas. But this is actually painful. What do I say?

"Err, thank you?"

"Oh, I'm sorry, I didn't mean to embarrass you," Evelyn says charmingly as she unhooks a bunch of keys from her neck and uses a tiny silver one to open the back of the glass cube displaying the cat rings.

She retrieves the dark-blue velvet tray holding the rings and sets it on a nearby glass cabinet. "These are our cat rings. They come in different materials, and are at different price points…"

Diego finally hovers next to me, listening in on Evelyn's explanation.

"…These ones here are all made of 10-carat gold: white, regular, and rose. And they cost $99.99." She opens a white drawer under the glass cabinet and takes out two small, blue velvet boxes, which contain two silvery rings. "These are sterling silver, our cheapest option at $29.99, and platinum, our most expensive at $499.99."

"Better get the cheapest one," Diego chimes in. "Can't

really tell the difference with the other ones."

Evelyn's next comment is cut off in a sort of gasp. "The materials may seem all the same right now, but the durability of platinum over time is superior by far. It's such a precious, timeless metal that will last a lifetime."

"Guess they can all make it to Christmas, though." Diego shrugs at her, and then, turning to me, he adds, "You can always tell your family it's platinum."

Gosh, he has *no* clue.

Evelyn's jaw has dropped to the floor by now, and I don't have the heart to look up at the other girls. I'm sure I'd find equally crestfallen faces. There's nothing I can say.

"Sterling silver it is," I offer lamely. "Can I try it on for sizes? I should be a six."

For a moment, Evelyn seems unable to speak. "A size six! Right," she manages at last, sounding strangled. "In sterling silver, lovely. So pretty."

She collects the right size and offers me the ring.

I slip it on my finger and… "It's a perfect fit."

"It is!" Evelyn is obviously forcing herself to nod animatedly. "So nice!" She exchanges looks with the other red girls, who all hastily chime in.

"Adorable!"

"Lovely choice!"

Their bright smiles *so* don't reach their eyes. One girl is actually blushing in mortification for me. I want to disappear.

"Would you like this gift wrapped?" Evelyn asks as she moves behind the register.

"Yes, please," I say.

"Maggie, can you take care of the wrapping?" she asks.

One of the girls shuffles close by and grabs the box,

careful to avoid looking me in the eye.

"With all our rings we also offer a care plan," Evelyn says. "For only ten dollars you get three cleanings and one re-sizing should you ever need it."

"A care plan on a thirty dollar ring?" Diego lets out an incredulous laugh. "That's such a rip-off."

"Just the ring," I hasten to say, before the situation gets any more awkward.

"Great." Evelyn taps the register keys, unfazed, almost anesthetized by Diego's lack of romanticism. "Would you be paying cash or credit, sir?" she asks Diego pointedly, her bright smile frozen solid.

Diego raises an eyebrow at me.

"Credit," I mutter, lowering my gaze to pull my credit card out of my wallet.

"So... you'll be paying for the ring, madam." She can barely gather control of herself. "Wonderful! That's... wonderful. No problem at all." Evelyn is breathing harder and harder. "Absolutely fine." She processes the payment and hands me the receipt to sign, still trying to keep the smile on. It's obviously taking up all her energy.

The other girl comes back with my package, her expression now openly aghast and hands it to me with an almost apologetic nod of support.

I'm under a hot shower of mortification. I nearly melt with embarrassment.

Diego, of course, has noticed nothing.

"We wish you both very happy holidays." Evelyn makes a supreme effort to stay pleasant as she ushers us to the door. But just as Diego walks out, she holds me back, pulling me by the elbow. "I know this is none of my business, hon," she whispers urgently in my ear. "But looks aren't everything, trust me."

As I finally exit the shop, Diego is waiting for me in the least over-packed corner of the hall, looking impatient.

"What was that about?" he asks. "Everything okay?"

"Yes! Super!"

I'm still flushed, and I just want to get out of this damned mall. A quick glance back toward the shop reveals Evelyn and the other girls talking animatedly and gesticulating out the window toward Diego with outraged looks on their faces.

"What's up?" Diego frowns. "That shop assistant seemed a little weird—"

"She was," I confirm, rolling my eyes.

Can he really be this clueless? Yes, he's a man. So I spell it out for him. "She thought you were my boyfriend making me buy my own Christmas present."

Light slowly dawns on Diego's face, and he bursts into laughter.

"So that's why they were all giving me the stink eye."

"Sorry, they all assumed you were a cheap bastard. I feel horrible."

Diego looks lost again. "Why? I don't care what three shop assistants think of me."

"Not even a bit?"

"Nope."

His face is relaxed, calm. He really doesn't care. How can he not care what other people think?

Well, that's probably why I'm the one hiring a fake boyfriend, and he's not.

Nine

A Purrfect Christmas

Mr. Fluff will run, jump, sit, and cuddle on request. He's a quick learner, and in just a few hours this magnificent exemplar of Silver Tabby British Shorthair can be trained to perform just about any task. At Le Paw Animal Talent Management Agency, we strive to provide our clients with the perfect animal for any job. We will provide you with expert advice and coordination to make all your productions spectacular.

I click on the casting video that shows Mr. Fluff playing with a plumed cat wand, chasing after a mechanical mouse... Then he eats, jumps, runs up the stairs, and the video ends with a close-up of the cat resting on a white couch while purring loudly. He seems indeed like a wonderful actor.

I grab the landline receiver and dial the agency number.

"Le Paw Animal Talent Management Agency," a female voice says, picking up on the second ring. "How can I help you?"

"Hi, hello, this is Nikki Moore from KCU Advertising. I was calling to inquire about one of your actors..." And, yes, I feel stupid saying this, but pet agencies can be a tad sensitive, and I've learned that if I don't refer to the animals as "professionals" or "talent" they can get pretty prickly. "Err... Mr. Fluff?"

"Oh, sure, Mr. Fluff is one of our best performers,

always in demand. Needs a month's advance booking at the very least."

"A month?" I gasp. "You mean he wouldn't be available this Thursday?"

"As in, the day after tomorrow?" the girl asks, appalled.

"Yes?"

"Sorry, ma'am. He's fully booked through January. Cats are very popular for Valentine's Day commercials, you know?"

Yes, I do know. It's my job to know. "Thank you very much anyway," I say, discouraged.

Third hole in the water today.

"You're welcome. And if you ever need our services in the future, don't hesitate to call us back. Le Paw Animal Talent Management Agency wishes you a purrfect Christmas."

Did she really just wish me a purrfect Christmas? I smash the receiver on its case three times, imagining it to be the face of the creative who suggested a tabby cat would suit the commercial better than the Russian Blue I'd hired.

It's Tuesday afternoon, and I'm losing a battle with time to wrap up this last-minute job that Teddy—my stupid holiday-loving boss—dumped on me. I'm about to click the link for the next animal "talent" agency when my personal phone starts vibrating somewhere on my desk. I can't see it; it must be hidden under some sheets of paper, so I ignore its insistent buzzing and let the call go unanswered. Five seconds later the vibration starts again, disrupting my concentration. If I keep ignoring whoever's calling, then curiosity would just bug me for the rest of the afternoon, slowing my progress even further. So I unceremoniously shuffle the piles of documents aside until I find the phone.

It's Blair.

Except for my "still alive" texts, we haven't talked much since she's moved out of the house, so I pick up.

"Hello?"

"Guess what I'm looking at right now?" she asks.

I sigh. "I don't have time for games, I'm swamped with work."

"Oh, what are you doing?"

"Watching cat videos. I'm trying to find a tabby cat that rolls on its back on command. Apparently, a monochrome gray cat doing everything exactly as it was told at every take wasn't pretty enough for the commercial we're shooting."

"You're watching cat videos and complaining?"

"It's not the cats; it's their trainers who drive me mad. Not to mention my creatives. So, are your eyes better occupied?"

"Oh, yeah. Right now I'm staring at the best six pack ever."

"Is Richard performing a mid-afternoon office striptease for you?"

"No, we hired Diego for the campaign." A vision of Diego clad only in a white towel flashes before my eyes, and I understand why Blair felt compelled to call me. Diego bare-chested is not an everyday sight. "The moment Angelika Black set eyes on him, it was game over for everybody else."

"Oh, great." I'm genuinely happy he got the job, and that, if nothing else, posing as my boyfriend will help his career. I guess one can't put "played fake boyfriend for a desperate single lady over the holidays" on one's résumé.

"So…" Blair says suggestively.

"So?"

"You've seen what I've seen?"

I can picture her waggling her eyebrows.

"Yes, it's in his portfolio," I lie. For some reason, I don't want her to know I had a real-life show. Two, counting the Santa World backstage.

"And?" she insists.

"And nothing."

"Are you telling me you're not even tempted?"

"To do what?"

"Oh, come on... You sleep in the candy shop every night, and you want me to believe you've never thought of tasting the candies?"

I massage my temples as the first signs of a cat-talent-plus-stupid-questions-from-my-best-friend induced headache start pressing on my skull. "Blair, we're in a *professional* agreement. I'm not going to hit on the guy." As if I had a chance, anyway. No matter what Diego says, guys like him don't end up with regular women like me.

"Why not? He's so hot, and he seems like a nice guy; couldn't you at least have some fun with this crazy pantomime of yours?"

"Why are you suddenly trying to push me into his arms? Only last week you were convinced he was a serial killer."

"Well..."

I can hear the guilt in her tone.

"Blair, what did you do?"

"Oh, nothing, really. But in order for us to hire him, he had to give us his social security number, and I told you how Richard wanted to meet the guy before we drove home with him... So, he sort of had a PI friend of his run a background check on Diego."

"You guys didn't," I hiss into the mic.

"We did, and you should thank us. Diego is squeaky clean. No criminal record, and his identity checked out. His credit score could be better, but that can be expected of a struggling artist."

"Oh my gosh." I close my eyes and intensify the massage. "He won't find out, will he?"

"I don't think so. And even if he does, we can always say it's a standard employee background check we carry out for all new hires."

"How wonderful," I say, hoping she'll catch the sarcasm.

"Stop being such a Scrooge. I just wanted to let you know that I approve."

"There's nothing to approve."

"If you say so. Anyway, that's not the only reason I called... Richard has booked his flight to London. Do you mind if we leave for home on Sunday instead of Saturday?"

"And skip a day in the torture pit? No, I don't mind."

"Okay, then. Richard will drop me and Chevron by the house early Sunday morning before he drives to the airport. Can you rent the car?"

"Sure, I'll book it when I get home from work." *If I ever leave this place,* I add in my mind. "When do you want to come back, on the twenty-ninth or the thirtieth?"

"Twenty-ninth?" Blair suggests. "So we get that extra day to recuperate before New Year's Eve?"

"Big plans?"

"No, just a party at Richard's friend's house. Want to come?"

"Is it all couples?"

"Err... I don't know. I can check if you want."

"Yeah, please." The last thing I need is to be the only sad loser at a party with no one to kiss at midnight. "So, I'll pick up the car Saturday night and schedule the drop off for the next Saturday." This way I can shave two whole days off my homestay and blame it on Blair and her British boyfriend with my mom. She loves Blair; she's not going to hold it against her. "A clean one-week rental. I hope they have discounts for that." Gosh, a full week at home. Fake boyfriend or not, the thought still makes me nauseous. "Anything else?"

"Just make sure the rental company allows for pets in the car."

"And maybe that they check their plates before doling out cars." I chuckle. "Wouldn't want to get arrested."

"Ah, ah... very funny."

"I'm still so sad they didn't take a mug shot of you," I say, referring to Blair's incident with law enforcement last summer. "I really gotta go now. See you on Sunday?"

"Yeah, bye."

"Bye."

***

Whenever I imagined low points in my career, delivering a sales pitch on all the qualities of Russian Blue cats never made the list. Nevertheless, the impossibility of finding a replacement "actor" forced me to do exactly that. I had to support my argument with adoption statistics, substantiated research on the most-loved cat breeds, and a small focus group's—made of the office secretaries—approval ratings for the specific cat performance.

In the end, I convinced the client to keep the Russian Blue. But this job is killing me. I have to treat myself to something, and since Diego and I also need more shared experiences, I ask Melanie to buy two tickets for *Harry Potter and the Cursed Child*. I'm sure Diego won't mind seeing it a second time.

When my assistant delivers the tickets to my desk the next day, she eyes me inquisitively. "Two front-row seats for tomorrow and Friday's shows," she says. "Solved that boyfriend issue, have you?"

I instantly regret having shared too much personal information with her. "Don't be ridiculous, I'm going with a friend."

"Oh, you seemed so much happier in the past week... I thought you'd met someone."

Happier, me? How, when I've been swamped by my usual workload, plus an impossible project, a rogue team of creatives, and had to deal with kitty-gate. I feel more stressed than ever, definitely not happier.

"What made you think that?" I ask.

"Nothing, really, but you seem more lively lately... more energetic. Usually happens to people who are in love."

"Didn't have much of a choice if I wanted to deliver everything Teddy asked for."

"Hey, don't get defensive, I was only saying you look better. Maybe it's the hair. Anyway..." She taps the tickets now resting on my desk, taking the hint my happiness level isn't a topic I care to discuss with her. "Both Part 1 and 2 start at 7:30 p.m. The ticket lady advised getting there a little early just to be on the safe side."

"Thank you, Mel, that'll be all," I dismiss her.

I stash the tickets away in my wallet and take a moment to stare out the window.

A CHRISTMAS DATE

I'm not happier.
Why would I be?

Ten

Bossy Much

The show is everything Diego promised. Definitely a much better experience than reading the script, and sharing it with him has made it even more special. The moment my fake boyfriend set foot on Broadway, his whole demeanor changed. The passion he has for the theater is contagious, and now I get why he can't surrender his dream and give up on being an actor. Getting a regular nine-to-five job would kill Diego's spirit. Pity it's so difficult to have a breakthrough in his field. I wish I could do something more to help him than sneak him into a few castings.

A frantic work schedule and two nights in a row spent on Broadway make the weekend and the imminent departure advance in no time. On Saturday, I indulge in a late morning and a lush brunch while Diego takes his last shift at the restaurant. Before I know it, it's time to get everything ready for the trip home. Come Saturday evening, I can't help feeling as jittery as an actor before opening night. Tomorrow, the biggest performance of my life will kick off, and no matter that all the technical details have been set, I'm still tense.

I do a mental recap.

Rental car, check!

Luggage packed and ready to be loaded, check!

Fake boyfriend, check!

But what about my nerves? Will I really be able to pull off this farce in front of my family? Will they believe Diego and I are together? I should've picked someone less hot than Diego; a guy more in my league. They're going to bust me the moment I step over the threshold. Why did I do this? This whole idea was crazy. I should call it all off.

No, no, Nikki, you just need to stop panicking and calm down.

Still, even with all the details of my fake relationship laid out, I can't settle. One final review can't hurt.

I sit on the coffee table in front of Diego, who's sprawled on the couch. I can tell he's tired after a day of waiting tables. But this won't take long.

"We should go over each other's backgrounds one last time," I announce.

"Boss, relax. We have it covered, went over it a million times."

"Also, you need to stop calling me 'boss.' When we're with my family, I'm Nikki."

"Or I could tell them I call you 'boss' for how bossy you are."

"I'm not bossy." I hand Diego his cheat sheet of information about my family and keep the one about his. "So, backgrounds."

"Bossy." He grins.

I scowl. "Be serious, we can't make mistakes. My family really needs to think we know each other."

Diego leans forward, dropping his elbows on his knees. "But we do, and better than most couples. We've been together all the time for two weeks." *Never this close, though.* His nose is only a few inches from mine. "Doesn't matter if you forget my third uncle's name."

"You think you know me?"

"I do."

"Prove it," I challenge him.

"Name: Nicola Addison Moore. Birthday: April 24. Born and raised in Old Saybrook. NYU graduate with a degree in Marketing and Visual design. Father: Jason Moore. Mother: Dora Moore, maiden name Appleton. Only one sibling, Julia, soon to be married to Paul Collins. And it doesn't matter if I don't remember your Aunt Laurel's middle name"—he pauses to peek at the sheet—"is Clara, and that she's the one allergic to nuts."

"It matters! You could offer her the wrong cookie and kill her," I say, somewhat annoyed that he's basically memorized the whole sheet, while I still struggle to remember all of his nephews' names.

"No, it doesn't. This list isn't that important; not when I've learned everything else about you."

"Like what?" I cross my arms pettily.

"You only have a few friends, but the ones you have, you would die for. Harry Potter is your favorite series, but you refuse to pick a single favorite book like everybody else because the story wouldn't exist without all seven novels. You never leave the house before spraying yourself head to toe in Flower by Kenzo, the same perfume you've used since you were sixteen..."

I gape at him. "How do you know that?"

"Blair told me." He winks.

Oh, so the two buggers talked about me behind my back.

"Anything else?" I ask.

"Yes. You like to paint your nails in the most obnoxious, shocking colors." I stare down at my fingers, and the tips are in fact neon pink. "But you'd never use a lipstick shade other than nude. Pity, because a bold red would look killer on you, if I may say."

"You may..." I mock-scold him.

Eyes never leaving mine, Diego continues, "You refuse to dress more casually at the office, even if your boss has probably told you a million times you could lie low on the suits..."

He has.

"...When you're concentrating, you reach out to twirl a lock of hair around your finger, only to lower your hand, disappointed, because you've forgotten you've chopped it all off..."

As he keeps talking, it's hard not to notice how green his eyes are, or how close our faces are hovering. Also hard to ignore is that, in just two weeks, he's mapped me out better than any boyfriend I've ever had. And I don't like the kind of fuzzy sensation his words are putting in my stomach, so I interrupt him, "Okay, you're very observant. Noted."

He leans back on the couch, arms behind his head, leaving a huge bubble of empty space in front of me. "Comes with the job," he says. "Every good actor needs to notice how other people behave."

Right. Remember, this is only a job for him. Also, I might need to take a cold shower.

I lift my butt from the coffee table and, pointing at the list in his hands, I say, "Just read it one more time before you go to bed. Blair will be here super early tomorrow morning."

"Aye, aye, boss."

"And stop calling me 'boss.'" I scowl again and am rewarded with a devilish grin.

Definitely need that cold shower.

***

At eight sharp the next morning, Blair walks into the apartment, Chevron in tow. Diego and I are just finishing a quick breakfast of coffee, milk, and cookies, when I'm assaulted by sixty pounds of enthusiastic dog.

"Yeah, yeah." I stroke Chevron behind the ears as she yaps away frantically, shaking her tail in a mad frenzy and trying to jump in my lap. "Good girl, I've missed you, too."

Diego leans against the kitchen bar column and eyes Chevron skeptically. "Is this supposed to be the trained attack dog?" he asks Blair.

"Hey," she says apologetically. "You were a perfect stranger living with my best friend. I had to use every possible form of intimidation."

Diego lets out two low whistles in sequence to attract Chevron's attention and crouches down.

Blair's dog, never one to shy away from cuddles or to be wary of strangers, responds to the call right away. She yaps happily and barrels into Diego with renewed enthusiasm, almost knocking him on his butt. Chevron keeps yapping for a while and then rolls on her back, paws in the air, offering her belly for Diego to pat.

"Well." Diego laughs. "If her strategy is to kill strangers with cuddles, she might succeed."

Twenty minutes later, we're in the car, me driving, Diego sitting shotgun, and Blair and Chevron in the backseat. We're heading north on FDR Drive toward Old Saybrook, and the traffic doesn't seem bad. We should get there in good time.

"So, Blair," Diego says, after a stretch of road spent in silence. "Are you, at least, happy to go home for the holidays?"

"Fifty percent," Blair replies.

Diego throws her a questioning look from the rearview mirror.

"I'm happy to see my dad," Blair explains, "but dreading seeing my mother."

"She a tough cookie?"

"More an insufferable snob, and she's not very happy with my latest life choices."

"Like?"

"Like quitting a career at a glossy magazine to work at a startup. And she's still trying to convince me that my cheating Manhattan lawyer ex was better than my perfect Brooklyn startup-owner boyfriend."

"Really? Why?" I insert myself into the conversation. "How can she?"

"Oh, you know Mrs. Walker, queen of suburbs living. Gerard is New York WASP old money elite, my mother's son-in-law wet dream."

"You should tell her Richard is royalty," I say. "That should shut her up."

"It probably would, but then she'd also expect to have tea with the Queen sooner or later, so you see how that could backfire."

At that moment, Blair's phone chimes, and she says, "Speaking of the devil, it's Richard."

"He's taking off?" I ask.

"No, says his flight is an hour late, and that he's ordering a coffee from my former suitor."

"What former suitor?"

"No idea," she says, and types away into the phone. "Ah," she yelps after a few seconds. "He's talking about Mark."

I've never heard of a Mark. "And who is this Mark

guy?"

"A cute bartender who works at JFK."

"Walker, you kept secrets," I mock-complain. "Why does Richard think this guy was your suitor?"

"Remember when we went to California last summer?"

"To Christian Slade's charity gala? Hell yeah. You flew off to meet the sexiest man alive and left me at home to take care of the furball."

"Woof," Chevron comments.

"You know Christian Slade?" Diego asks, visibly impressed. Guess that kind of fame is like the oasis mirage in the desert for him.

"My boyfriend does. They went to boarding school together back in England. Anyway, Richard and I weren't together at the time," she explains to Diego, "and I was so nervous about going on a trip with my boss—"

"Who she had a huge crush on," I intervene.

"Who I had a huge crush on," Blair confirms. "That I poured my heart out to this bartender guy, and we became sort of friends, and Richard—"

"Who was in denial about not having feelings for her back then," I helpfully supply.

"—who was in denial about not having feelings for me back then, thought I was flirting with the guy. Should I tell him the whole discussion was about him?"

I say, "No," just as Diego says, "Yes."

"Explain yourselves, both of you," Blair orders.

"Keep Richard on his toes," I say. "Make him see how lucky he is you're with him."

"Diego?" Blair asks.

"You guys are in a serious relationship?"

"Yeah."

"He loves you, and you love him?"

"Mmm-hmm."

"No need to play games, then. For a guy, what you say is what you mean. If you say you were flirting with this dude, Richard will believe you. He won't think you were really obsessing over him the whole time, and only telling him it was a flirt to *keep him on his toes...*" Diego throws me an overcritical side stare. "He's not going to realize how lucky he is to have you; he'll just assume you weren't that into him at the time of the trip. My suggestion is to tell the truth and give the guy's ego a little boost. You'll send him to London happy with a big, goofy smile on his face."

I hear Blair tapping on the phone and narrow my eyes at her in the rearview mirror. "Are you taking his advice over mine?"

She shrugs. "He's a guy."

Her phone chimes back a second later.

"So, what did Richard say?" I ask.

"Sent me the 'cool' emoji with the sunglasses, and a shower of kisses, and says he loves me."

"I'm getting diabetes," I say, smiling, and change the subject. "Before we get home, you need to be up to date on our narrative."

"What narrative?" Blair asks.

"How Diego and I met, our first date, how long we've been together, and so on..."

"Oh, so we're not telling people you picked him off a catalog?" she jokes.

"Blair, be serious, you have to memorize everything we tell you, and we only have about two hours."

She pokes her head between the front seats to speak to Diego. "Don't you hate her when she's this bossy?" she asks him.

His only response is to throw back his head and let out a throaty laugh.

This is going to be the longest week of my life.

Eleven

There's No Place Like Home for the Holidays

Too soon for my cranky nerves, I'm pulling onto my street. The neighborhood in which Blair and I grew up resembles the perfect Christmas dream fairy tale at this time of the year—or nightmare, depending on one's feelings toward the holidays. Rows and rows of perfectly-curated townhomes and gardens coated in dusty snow, mercilessly decorated to the death.

My house, in particular, could win the go-absolutely-nuts-with-fairy-lights competition. There isn't a single tree or shrub that isn't supporting some kind of illumination contraption. And on the lawn, they've scattered sparkly reindeers and a huge light-up sleigh. Even in daylight, the house is blinding, I wonder what it'll do at night. Guess my mom ran off the bat with her daughters bringing home a fiancé and a new boyfriend, respectively.

I kill the car's engine and turn back toward Blair. "Here we are." She lives just across the street. "Are you coming over tonight after dinner?"

"Definitely," Blair says, clipping on Chevron's leash.

"All right." I button up my coat, and we all get out of the car.

Diego helps Blair unload her bag and does the same with ours.

"Say hello to your parents," Blair says, hugging me. "See you later."

I watch her cross the street and then turn back toward my house, filled with dread.

I look up at Diego. "Ready?"

He nods.

"Let's do this."

I hook my travel bag over my shoulder next to my regular bag and walk up the driveway to the porch. My gloved finger has barely touched the doorbell when the door swings open to reveal Mom, Dad, and Julia crowding the threshold. If Diego was a real boyfriend, and not one paid to endure my family, I'd be dying of shame at their ill-concealed eagerness. Mom and Julia look like wolfhounds with the scent of a bone fresh in their nostrils.

Mom is poring over Diego in awe. I don't think she even notices how hot he is; she's just overwhelmed he's the first boyfriend I've brought home since high school. Julia, on the other hand, is staring at him slightly slack-jawed. Ah, ah. Bet she was expecting me to introduce them to someone boring and possibly balding, not Mr. Tall, Dark, and Mysterious. Take that, little sis.

"Hi, everyone," I greet them, walking inside and taking notice of how the interior of the house is no better than the outside. Looks like a Christmas Tree Shop has opened in here. Every square inch is covered with a decoration, wreath, or Christmas light, and the tree they bought this year is so massive it almost touches the living room ceiling. "Mom, Dad, this is Diego," I make the introductions. "Diego, this is my mom, dad, and my sister, Julia."

They all do the "nice to meet you" handshake dance— or, at least, my parents do. Julia just stares at Diego, speechless, as he shakes her hand.

Something brushes against my legs, and I bend down to pick up the only being I'm actually excited to see over this break: Mr. Darcy, the family tomcat. Dad found him hiding under his truck when he was just a tabby kitten in my junior year of high school. Even if we only lived under the same roof for two years, I still consider him my cat. In fact, the moment he's in my arms, he starts purring and bumping his head under my chin.

In the three seconds I've been distracted by Mr. Darcy, my mom has closed in on Diego and is bombarding him with questions.

"Mom," I interrupt her, saving him. "Let us at least drop our bags before you start with the third degree."

Then I make the mistake of using my cat-free hand to pull my beanie off.

Mom gasps. "Darling, your hair!"

Oh, I forgot they haven't seen my new haircut yet.

"Yeah." I ruffle it up to remove the flattening effect of the hat. "New style."

"But your hair was so pretty."

Mom uses the same tone she'd strike up if someone in the family had died.

"Well, I wanted something different. I need to drop these off," I say, tilting my chin toward the bags dangling from my side. Between them and the cat, who's no feather-weight, my arms are getting heavy. "Can we discuss how I ruined my hair later?"

"That's not what I meant, honey, of course you look gorgeous."

Dad takes the opportunity to give me a side hug. "Love the new cut, baby."

"Thanks, Dad." I kiss him on the cheek. "So, we'll pop upstairs and be right back."

"Great," Mom says. "Lunch is almost ready. You two go freshen up and come back downstairs whenever you're ready. But don't take too long," she adds in a shrill voice. "I've made mac and cheese, and it needs to come out of the oven soon."

Diego gives her the perfect future-son-in-law answer. "Can't wait to taste it, Mrs. Moore. I've been told your cooking is the best in the entire state."

He's worth every single penny.

Mom blushes, and coos, "Oh, please, it's just something I threw together in five minutes." She's lying. Her secret recipe for mac and cheese requires at least five different cheeses and a complicated double-baking timing. And sometimes, besides baked breadcrumbs, she also adds shrimp or lobster, which of course she has to cook separately first, and then add later in the oven. Hardly a five-minute meal. "And please, call me Dora," she concludes.

"I will." Diego flashes her a bright smile, making his conquest final and absolute.

Mom scurries back to the kitchen happier than I've seen her in years.

"This way." I guide Diego up the stairs, still holding Mr. Darcy in my arms.

On the landing, my heart almost stops as I find myself face-to-face with Paul.

"I heard some noises," he says, smiling, his blue stare piercing a hole through my soul. "Thought you might've arrived." Then his eyes widen. "New haircut, huh? Looks great on you."

I try not to blush, and keep a detached, sister-in-law-appropriate tone. "Paul," I greet him, and give him a quick hug, squishing Mr. Darcy between us. My nostrils immediately fill with his cologne; he was wearing CK One the first day I met him, and I've never smelled anything else on him. Guess we both stick to a perfume when we find one we like. "You guys got here last night, right?"

"Yeah."

"Have my parents scared you off already?" I joke.

"Nuh-uh."

"Not even the princess bed?"

Paul grins. "That almost did it, but IKEA saved me. We shipped a bed and mattress here before leaving New York, and we assembled everything yesterday."

"Oh, I never thought Julia would give up her pink castle."

"Your dad and I brought it down to the garage. The decision on what to do with it is still pending."

"What are the options?"

"Your parents want to give it away to charity, but Jules point-blank refuses. She wants to keep it in case we have a daughter."

Ice courses through my veins. "You guys are... mmm... expecting?"

"What? No!" Paul laughs the question off, and I can breathe again. "She's just thinking future tense; *way* future tense."

"Err-hem," Diego clears his throat behind me.

I had completely forgotten he was here.

"Oh, right." I turn sideways in the hall to give him room to climb the last two steps. "Paul, this is Diego, my boyfriend. Diego, Paul, Julia's soon-to-be husband."

Another handshake, and Paul is on his way downstairs.

So far so good. Operation "Fake Boyfriend" is proceeding well. Nobody looked at Diego and me and screamed "Imposters!"

In my room, I drop Mr. Darcy on the bed, the bags on a chair, and finally remove my coat. I was overheating; it must be eighty degrees in the house. Once Diego is inside, I close the door behind him and whisper, "What do you think?"

He looks at me sheepishly. "Of what?"

"Did they look suspicious?"

"Relax, b—" I give him such a fierce scowl that he changes words mid-sentence. "Nikki. We've talked to them for only five minutes. No one suspects anything."

I take his jacket and hang it next to mine. "Good. Great job buttering up my mom," I say. "Nicely done."

He grins. "Hey, I have a mom, I know how to handle those. Your sister is a different story, though, she didn't seem to warm up to me."

"Julia was probably just surprised." I do an evil laugh inside my head. Yeah, surprised that her dream man just materialized before her eyes as my boyfriend. "You're not exactly my type."

"You have a type?"

Yes. Tall, blond, blue eyes... engaged to my sister...

"I do."

"And why am I not it?"

Because you're not Paul.

"You're too dark," I say instead, gesturing at his hair.

"So why pick me again?"

"You had the best face, I've already told you."

"So I was chosen solely because of my face?" He gives me a long and penetrating stare, prompting quick flashes of the other photos in his portfolio—where his face definitely played the extra—to invade my mind.

I break eye contact and manage to mumble, "Among

your other very respectable assets."

"Oh, so now I have assets?" He chuckles. "What assets?"

"You know, stuff?"

"What stuff?"

I huff, exasperated. "You have a nice ass, happy?"

"Very." He laughs. "Likewise, boss."

I hide my blush with an angry pout. "Don't call me 'boss.'"

"All right, all right. You want to go downstairs?"

"No?"

I'm terrified.

"Well, unless you want your family to think you're up here playing with some of my *assets*... we'd better go."

I try to ignore the sexy pun, even if my cheeks heat up, and ask, "Are you ready? Do you remember everything?" I fire one nervous question after the other. "Do you need to meditate? Take a few moments to get into character?"

"I've had two weeks to get into character. I'm ready if you are."

"Okay." I hold out my hand and he takes it. It's nothing romantic, just human solidarity. Even if his hand is warm and dry and really big and it feels kind of good in mine. "Let's go do this."

And shame on me because, as we exit the room, I peek behind my shoulder at the reflection of my butt in the wardrobe mirror. I never thought of myself as a nice-ass girl; I never really gave my buns much consideration. Still, there's nothing I can do to hide the small, satisfied smile that hasn't left my lips since Diego's comment.

When we arrive downstairs, everyone is already seated at the dining table and gossiping—probably about us, seeing how the conversation dies off the second Diego and I enter the room. Could they be any more obvious?

Mom and Dad are sitting at opposite heads of the table, with Julia and Paul occupying one of the long sides between them. So I sit next to Dad in front of Julia, and Diego takes the seat next to Mom, facing Paul.

An embarrassed silence lingers for about thirty seconds before my mom gets up. "Everyone's here," she says, moving toward the kitchen. "I'll go get the food."

In sixty seconds she's back with a steaming oven dish filled to the brim with delicious and super-creamy-looking mac and cheese.

And, yes, the lobster and breadcrumbs topping. Yum!

Mom sets the dish in the center of the table and disappears back into the kitchen, returning with a smaller, round dish that she lays in front of Julia. My sister's special preparation seems like a smaller tureen of mac and cheese, but the color is slightly off—a sad, dirty white instead of rich cream—and there is no lobster or breadcrumbs on top. Also, the pasta is different; looks kind of gummy.

"You having a different menu?" I ask Julia.

"The wedding is in only six months; I'm on a vegan diet until then."

"You're vegan? Since when?"

"Since I need a pre-wedding detox. For the next semester, I've sworn off meat, dairy, seafood, sugar, gluten, and all other poison foods."

"Good for you," I say, trying to keep the sarcasm from my voice and doing my best not to roll my eyes. Secretly, I'm thanking the Christmas spirits she hasn't convinced Mom to cook the vegan version of her mac and cheese for everyone.

"Guests first," my mom chimes in. Eager to end the vegan discussion, I'm sure. She serves Paul and Diego, and then me and Dad. "Well, everyone, enjoy your meal... Bon appétit!"

"Bon appétit," we all reply. Well, all except for Diego, who goes for a slightly different version, saying, *"Buon appetito."*

"Is that Italian I hear, young man?" Dad asks.

"Yes, sir, I'm part Italian from my mother's side."

"Please, call me Jason," my dad says. "So, you speak Italian?"

"Bene come l'Inglese." Diego smiles.

"Oh," Julia gasps. "I've always wanted to learn Italian."

I think of my sister's secret list of qualities for her perfect man, and mentally check off "speaks Italian." I should also check off tall, dark, and with smoldering green eyes. She's seen that.

"So, Diego, what is it that you do in New York?" my mom asks. "Nikki hasn't told us much."

"I'm an actor," Diego replies.

The declaration is followed by a prolonged moment of silence.

"An actor?" my dad repeats. "What kind of acting?"

"Theater on Broadway would be the dream, of course, but for now I scrape by with whatever I can get. Commercials, modeling... Christmas is always good, so many Santa gigs are available."

"Y-you play Santa at the mall?" my mom asks.

My parents are still a bit too "middle class" for this kind of future-son-in-law. I'd feel sorry for them, if not for the years of pestering me about settling down. This is like a small, sweet revenge.

115

"Yeah, but I mainly work as a server to pay the bills. Until my big break comes, I'm living paycheck to paycheck."

Julia is openly gaping right now. I mentally check "struggling artist" off the list. I can't wait for Diego to tell her he rides a motorcycle.

Dad, on the other hand, isn't impressed. "How old are you?" he asks.

Guess we're not over the "lack of a proper enough career to date my daughter" topic.

"Twenty-eight," Diego answers.

"And do many actors have big breaks when they're close to thirty? I thought they all had to start much earlier..."

"Depends on—"

"Diego's job is actually how we met," I interrupt. "We bumped into each other at the agency." Then, wanting to make it clear the third degree is over—I might be paying Diego, but no one deserves to be grilled this hard—I turn to Mom. "Mom, you've outdone yourself. It's like your mac and cheese gets better every year."

"Yeah, truly delicious." Paul and Diego echo my compliments. "Amazing recipe."

"And how is yours?" I ask Julia.

She narrows her eyes at me. "Healthier, for sure."

Uh-oh, someone sounds a little sour...

Twelve

Better Eat Your Vegetables

Luckily, lunch continues with no further interrogations. But when the meal's over and everyone has had coffee—except for Julia, who opted for a fennel infusion—I've already had enough of the family reunion, so I take the excuse of showing Diego around town to get the hell out of the house.

"Congratulations, you survived the first drill," I tell Diego as we exit the car and stroll toward the town's center.

Downtown is not that impressive, just a road with shops and restaurants on either side. But with the snow crunching under our feet and fairy lights dangling from every tree and shop window, I have to admit the Christmas flourish makes it prettier than usual.

"Mmm, I don't think your dad was a fan of my job," Diego says, offering me his arm.

"Don't worry, he won't have time to try to turn you into an accountant," I reassure him, linking our arms together. "Five more days and you'll never see him again."

"Right." Diego's face doesn't look relieved.

"Come on, I promise I'll keep my dad off your back." I pull him toward the main shopping street. "Ready to dive into my past?"

Diego nods and follows me obligingly around town as I show him all the local attractions.

***

"And I worked at that café for two years when I was sixteen to eighteen," I say about half an hour later. I kept my favorite coffee house for last. "Hot chocolate? They make the best in town with melting marshmallows and a side of cookies."

Diego rubs his hands in a warming gesture. "You had me at *hot*."

Old Saybrook is only two hours north of Manhattan, but the climate is considerably more frigid up here; even a short time outside is enough to freeze one's ass over.

I push my way into the shop, making the little bell over the door chime in greeting. If the atmosphere was Christmassy outside, in here it looks like a drunken elf threw up all over the place. But not even the Christmas overload and cheesy tunes can keep me from enjoying the best chocolate ever brewed.

"Nikki," Mrs. Cravath, my former employer, greets me. "So good to see you! And who is this young man?" She eyes Diego from behind the counter with sparkly eyes.

"Hello, Mrs. Cravath. This is Diego, my boyfriend," I introduce.

"Oh, how wonderful. See? I was right, and they were wrong," she says, and I have absolutely no clue what she's talking about. "Dora owes me one of her famous pumpkin pies."

"Excuse me?" I say.

"Your mom and your old crone of an aunt always complain you're never going to find a man. But I told them how wrong they were and bet Dora a pie you'd be married before forty, which is the new thirty." She winks at me.

Again, if Diego really was my boyfriend, I'd be dead from the shame. Now I'm just livid. I'm not sure what makes me angrier: the fact that my mom openly discusses my dating life with the whole town or that, apparently, the prize of my happiness is a pumpkin pie. I'm almost tempted to turn on my heel and get the hell out, but then I get a whiff of cacao and can't help myself. No gossiping old ladies will keep me from my hot chocolate.

"Still ten years to go," I point out, putting on a sterner and definitely less cordial tone. "I'm sure you'll get your pie, eventually." I rejoice in knowing that my lifelong spinsterhood will at least deprive Mrs. Cravath—who I honestly liked until five minutes ago—of her pie.

"So, what can I get you two lovebirds?" she asks, unaware of my shifted demeanor.

"We'll take two hot chocolate specials, thank you."

"Go sit... I'll be right there with your order."

We choose a table by the window, and I can't help but notice how Diego's mouth keeps twitching.

"You have something to add?" I hiss.

"No, sorry." He finally lets the smile dance on his lips. "It's just that I grew up in Chicago, and now I live in New York..."

"So?" I ask, impatient.

"I never got that whole 'small town where everyone knows everyone' thing. But now I do."

"Welcome to my personal ho-ho-hell." I roll my eyes. "See why I needed you here?"

"I'm starting to."

***

When we leave the café, it's already dark outside. We hop into the car and I take Diego to the final spot of our tour.

We cross a stretch of open water toward Lynde Point, and I pull over on the other side of the bridge. "Our famous lighthouse is over there, but I can't get any closer with the car. Want to take a stroll? It's really pretty at night."

"Sure," Diego says.

I open the car door, and a freezing blizzard attacks me. "On second thought," I say, pulling the door close again. "It's too windy out there. Another day?"

"At least we'll still have an excuse to get out of the house." He grins.

"I see you're getting into the right Christmas spirit." I glance at the car's clock. "Oh, and it's late, anyway. My parents like to eat dinner early."

Diego massages his belly. "If dinner is anything like lunch, I'm all in. Your mom is an amazing cook."

"Yeah." I reverse the car and hit the road again. "The food is one of the few perks of coming home for the holidays."

As we drive, I keep up my role of improvised tour guide whenever we pass a building of interest, like the local brewery, or the Katharine Hepburn museum and the cultural arts center. "And that's my high school," I say, pointing. "And right there, under the ledge near the entrance, is where I had my first kiss."

"And who was the lucky guy?"

"Michael Connell, a real jackass. The jerk dumped me for Rebecca Miller three weeks later."

"Ouch."

"Yeah, my first heartbreak. Took me a whole month to get over him," I joke. "What about you? Who broke your heart for the first time?"

"Ah, freshman year. Sally Parker agreed to come to the

school dance with me only because her parents knew me, then she ditched me to go make out with a senior all night."

"So, you weren't a ladies' man in high school?"

Looking at him now, I find it hard to believe.

"I was a late bloomer. In the ninth grade, I was your typical skimpy kid: skinny and short. Then the summer between freshman and sophomore year I shot up a foot and started playing basketball, packed on some muscle."

"Did Sally Parker ever regret her decision?"

Diego shrugs. "Don't think so. We never talked much after that night."

I don't know why, but I'm pretty sure old Sally *did* curse herself for not sticking with the ugly duckling until he turned into a swan.

***

When we get back home, the house smells like kale and rotten eggs.

"Mom," I call. "We're back."

"Great." She comes out of the kitchen, looking a little frazzled. "Dinner is almost ready."

"Yeah, what is this smell? What did you make?"

"Your sister…" She lowers her stare to the floor for a second before answering. "She's offered to cook us dinner tonight."

"Julia's cooking?" I ask, horrified.

"She swears we could all use the detox, and she's put a lot of effort into making dinner, so don't you dare be nasty about it."

Of course, we wouldn't want to hurt poor Julia's feelings.

"Now, go sit at the table," Mom orders.

Filled with dread, I step into the dining room and stare at the laid table, aghast.

I quickly turn toward Diego and whisper in his ear, "I'm really sorry for what's about to happen. Please pretend you still like me after this."

But if anyone wanted to know what real terror looks like, they should watch my father's face as Julia presents our multi-course vegan dinner. To my credit, I'm trying to keep a neutral expression, as is Diego, while Paul has the resigned look of someone who has listened to this speech multiple times. The only one showing an ounce of enthusiasm is Mom.

Jules is lecturing us on all the benefits of abandoning unhealthy eating habits to cleanse our bodies of toxins, clear our minds of food-induced headaches, and save our stomachs from bloating... and our arteries from clogging... and our skin from breaking out... and on, and on, and on...

I've lost count of all the damages I'm inflicting on my person with my daily diet when my dad asks, "But is a little meat really that bad?"

"Yes, Dad," Julia confirms. "Do you know that we have an herbivorous digestive system, and not carnivorous?"

"Aren't we omnivorous?" he asks, hopeful.

"Not in origin. In fact, the human intestine is twenty-eight feet long. A lion, for example, only has ten feet. A long intestine is a characteristic of herbivorous animals. That's why we can't digest meat properly. It takes too long for it to journey through our guts, and it starts to putrefy while it's still inside our bodies. And I don't know about you, but I prefer to keep my intestines free of rotting corpses."

"Sure, honey," Dad concedes, defeated.

I don't even want to know where she gets her information. And from the various expressions around the table ranging from disgust to despair, it seems my fellow diners are of the same mind.

When the introductory speech is over, Julia finally presents the first course: pumpkin soup with chia seeds.

Pumpkin soup doesn't sound that bad; I love soup. As Julia sets the bowl before me, I'm even encouraged by the color: a deep, rich orange. And the smallish brown seeds she's used as a garnish don't seem too scary. I'm actually kind of enthusiastic as I grab my spoon to have a taste.

When everyone is served, Julia claps her hands. "Tuck in, everyone."

I take a large spoonful, and wince. "Julia," I protest. "The soup is cold."

"It's not cold, it's lukewarm," she says, her tone of voice implying I just said something really stupid.

"Well, I prefer my soup hot," I say, getting up. "I'll microwave it real quick. Does anyone else want me to microwave theirs—"

"You can't microwave it!" Julia shouts. I freeze in place as she explains, "First of all, microwaves are really toxic." She turns toward Mom. "You should get rid of that death trap." Her focus shifts back to me. "And second, you can't warm the pumpkin. Keep it at two hundred degrees for even a minute and you lose half of all the thermolabile vitamins."

"I think I can live with fewer vitamins if it means I can eat hot soup."

"Suit yourself, but that's not how it's supposed to be eaten. You might as well go out and order a burger."

That actually sounds like a great idea.

"Why don't you give Julia's cooking a try," my mom

intervenes. "She's put so much effort into preparing this lovely dinner for all of us." She gives me a long, now-be-good-and-eat-your-disgusting-cold-soup stare.

I sit back down, resigned, and do my best to force a few more spoonfuls of this cold poultice down my throat. Cold soup in December! This is a madhouse.

Unfortunately, the main course—tofu steak—doesn't prove any tastier or more filling. The only saving grace is the salad side. Not really much you can do wrong with a salad, even if Dad isn't allowed to use his favorite ranch dressing as it has dairy in it, which is supposedly even worse than meat. Cow Milk & Co are guilty of containing lactose—we don't possess the enzymes to digest it—as well as casein, a dreadful animal protein capable of causing cancer, respiratory problems, inflammation, bloating, headaches...

Makes me wonder if at the agency we should put side-effect warnings at the end of our food commercials like we do with pharmaceuticals.

As for me, I'm happy I'm allowed to use olive oil to dress the salad, even if the salt gets rationed down—it's bad for blood pressure.

The cherry on the cake of the most horrible dinner ever is the dessert: an oatmeal pudding made with maca root powder, so dense it has the consistency of glue. Of course, not a pinch of sugar in it.

I really try to finish mine, but I can't; each tiny spoonful I ingest makes me want to gag more than the previous one. Diego, definitely a much better sport, manages to finish all his pudding, and even has the poker face to compliment Julia, gaining an appreciative nod from my mom.

And so, after an hour and a half of suffering, we're all allowed to retire for the night and go lick our wounds in private. I don't know if this is a behavior typical of herbivorous or carnivorous species, but right now, I'm only hoping I can find a cereal bar hidden at the bottom of my bag.

Thirteen

Pizza Gate

Later, in my room, Diego and I are lying on opposite sides of the bed, wrapped in utter misery. Mr. Darcy, who wasn't forced to eat a vegan cat dinner, is curled up at our feet, much more contented. Barely half an hour since we left the dinner table and I'm already famished. So much so that my stomach grumbles loudly, prompting Diego to turn toward me.

"Hungry?" he asks.

"Yeah, you?"

"Starving. Does your mom have any of that mac and cheese left?"

"Even if she did, we can't go downstairs and heat it up in the evil microwave. If Julia found out, she'd throw the tantrum of the century."

"Right now, I'd gladly eat it cold."

"Nah, I've had enough cold food for one night." I sigh as my belly complains again.

I can't go to sleep on an empty stomach. There must be a way to get a proper dinner without Julia finding out...

"Wait," I say, and grab my phone to text Blair.

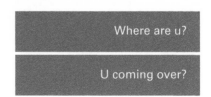

Where are u?

U coming over?

A CHRISTMAS DATE

Yeah, just finishing walking Chevron

Be there in ten

Any chance you'll pass near the pizza place by the corner?

Standing right in front of it now

Why?

Can you order two giant pizzas to go?

Sure

I ♥ you

When you get here come in through the back door

It's open

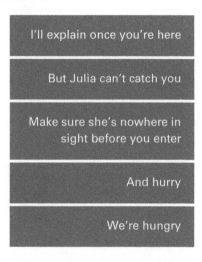

Come upstairs immediately and be stealthy

No one can see you

???

I'll explain once you're here

But Julia can't catch you

Make sure she's nowhere in sight before you enter

And hurry

We're hungry

Half an hour later the door of my room bursts open and Blair enters in a blur, balancing two giant pizza boxes in one hand while trying not to stumble over Chevron. The dog has barreled into the room, slaloming between her legs.

"I've made it," she says.

I get up to relieve her of the pizzas, and carefully close the door behind her.

"Did anyone see you?" I ask.

"Your dad, but he's promised to keep quiet." Blair bites her lower lip. "But I suspect he might come over and ask for a pizza bribe in exchange for his silence. He was looking at the boxes like he's never seen pizza before. Did you guys all skip dinner or something?" She removes her coat and goes to sit at my desk.

I jump back on the bed, handing Diego a box and opening mine while Chevron sniffs every corner of the room. When she gets near the bed to sniffle out Mr. Darcy, the cat's only reaction is to lift his head and throw the dog a disdainful stare. Subdued by this display of animal hostility, Chevron lets out a low whine and settles on the rug by the bed.

Before answering Blair, I can't resist a quick bite of pizza. It tastes delicious. The place by the corner makes a thick dough and always puts loads of extra cheese—*real, made with milk that came from cow's cheese*—on top. But it's not just that; this pizza is the taste of my youth. I can't even remember how many Blair and I shared over the years.

When my grumbling stomach is somewhat placated, I finally show enough restraint to stop scarfing down pizza and talk. "Worse than skipping dinner," I explain. "Julia cooked."

"Oh, is she that bad?"

"No idea, but tonight she made us a vegan meal." I switch my tone of voice to talk like a yoga teacher. "To help us cleanse our bodies before the coming days of unchecked indulging." I go back to my normal voice. "And half of it was *raw* vegan cuisine, in the middle of December. Can you believe it?"

"Mmm... But you like it when I make you vegetarian dinners..."

"Yeah, because A, you can cook, and B, you actually cook your vegetables. Plus, vegan is extreme: no cheese, no eggs, no butter. And she only allowed gluten-free bread. The entire dinner was disgusting, and we were both hungry again half an hour later."

Blair laughs. "Yes, I guess vegan eating can be hard."

"Thanks for the pizzas." Diego lifts a slice toward her as if he was toasting a glass of wine. "You're a life saver."

"Wouldn't want anyone to starve." She smiles, then lowers her voice conspiratorially. "So, how did today go? Did 'the family' buy your story?"

I'm about to reply when there's a knock on the door and my dad quickly sneaks into the room.

"Ah." I look at him. "Come to exact payment for your silence, I see."

Dad puts on an innocent face that doesn't reach his mischievous, twinkly eyes. "Would you refuse an old man a slice of pizza?"

"Here." I grab a napkin and place a big slice on top, handing it to him.

And, old man or not, he looks like an excited kid as he takes it from me.

Dad hasn't finished his first bite when the door opens again and Paul slips inside, clearing his throat. "Err... I heard there was black-market pizza here."

I throw a killer stare at my dad, who promptly justifies himself. "Found him in the kitchen scavenging for food. Couldn't let the poor fella starve."

I roll my eyes and hand them my box with the remaining half of my pizza. Diego, the saint, nudges his box toward me and I gladly take another slice.

That's when Mom arrives. She stares at us, asking, "What are you all doing up here?"

Why no one ever knocks in this house...?

Dad swiftly ushers her inside and closes the door behind her. "Shhh, Dory. You want to get us caught?"

Mom scowls at him. "Your daughter worked so hard to cook you dinner, and if she were to find you all eating pizza behind her back she'd be crushed."

Dad keeps eating, unperturbed. "And that's why I ate my dinner in silence like a good father would. But if my other daughter decides to sneak pizza into the house later, it's only fair I accept all of my offsprings' culinary offerings."

"Two dinners are too much at your age," my mom insists.

"Oh, come on, Dory dear. Only a slice." He turns the open box toward her tantalizingly. "Get one yourself and relax; it's Christmas."

Mom stares at the pizza for a while, indecision clearly written on her features. She's just reaching for the slice when the door opens again and Julia enters, saying, "Nik, do you know where everyone went?"

We all freeze, caught in the act.

Julia takes in the scene, and her jaw drops just before her eyes go all watery. "If you didn't like dinner, you could've said so," she wails dramatically. Then her gaze narrows on Mom, who's standing immobile, arm still stretched forward, reaching for the box. "I could've expected it from them." Julia points at me and my dad. "But I hoped for better from you." Then she turns toward Paul, points an accusing finger at him, and hisses, "And you."

With that, she turns on her heel and flees the room. Mom retracts her arm and runs after her. "Julia, baby... Wait."

Paul, on the other hand, shrugs and serenely finishes his

slice. "She'll get over it," he reassures us, before going after his fiancée.

Dad, equally nonplussed, says, "Well, since we've been busted, I can go finish this downstairs." And he, too, leaves, bringing the pizza box with him.

"So," Blair says, when it's only the three of us left in the room—five, counting pets. "I guess it's been a regular day in the Moore family and no one suspects anything."

"Pretty much," I confirm. "What about you? How were your parents?"

We complain about our respective families for another hour or so, before Blair lets out a very loud yawn. "Sorry, guys. I'm beat. Time to go home."

"I'll walk you downstairs," I say.

She and Diego say goodnight while I check the hallway to make sure my sister isn't around. I know she'll make me pay for the pizza stunt, and I'm not looking forward to the moment she'll decide to take her revenge. Luckily, she seems to have already retired to bed, and Blair and I don't meet anyone on our way to the front door.

"How much do I owe you for the pizzas?" I ask, unhooking my bag from the entrance rack.

"Oh, please. Pizza's on me tonight."

"Are you sure?"

"Yeah. Good night, honey. I'll see you tomorrow."

We exchange a quick hug, and I'm about to draw away when she pulls me back in to whisper in my ear, "Oh, and enjoy your first night in bed with Diego." There's plenty of mischief in her voice.

"Blair," I hiss, outraged. "It's not like that."

"I'm just saying that if your hands happened to wander a little under the sheets in the middle of the night, no one could really blame you."

"Only sue me for sexual harassment."

Blair finally lets me go and, with a wink, she adds, "You should try to have more fun."

I shoo her out of the house without comment, taking a moment afterward to rest my back against the door, her words still ringing in my ears. Am I nervous about sleeping in the same bed with Diego? A little... but we're both adults and professionals. The situation might be awkward, but we don't have to make a big fuss about it.

When I get back upstairs, Diego is not in the room. He probably followed me downstairs to go to the bathroom to get ready for the night. He and Paul are using the guest bathroom downstairs, while Julia and I share the one on this floor, and my parents have an en suite.

Did he overhear Blair and me talking? No, impossible. We were whispering.

While he's gone, I shed my clothes at the speed of light and quickly change for bed, feeling glad I opted to bring un-sexy, warm PJs. The thought of bringing lacy lingerie instead *had* crossed my mind as I was packing, but then I decided that my butt would've frozen in skimpy underwear. And, honestly, the embarrassment of wearing close to nothing in front of Diego would've been too much. And anyway, it's not like I have to seduce him or anything.

The door opens, and he walks in wearing only a black T-shirt and gray sweatpants—guess he doesn't need special lingerie to look hot.

He eyes my outfit, the corners of his mouth curling up. "You're sleeping in that?"

I stare down at my plush black hoodie, complete with kitty ears, and the matching mint leggings covered in a black cat print. "Yes, why? You don't like it?"

Diego shakes his head. "Actually," he says, as if he can't believe his own words, "it's kind of cute."

So now I'm cute?

No, Nikki, the PJs are cute, not you.

Right.

"Well, thanks," I mumble, trying not to blush. "And you're sleeping in that?" I ask, pointing at his clothes.

"I don't usually keep the sweatpants on, but I can tonight if it bothers you. I mean, am I even sleeping in the bed?"

"Mmm, yeah, where else would you sleep?"

"I thought you might send me to the floor."

"No, no. There's plenty of space in the bed, unless you... want to sleep on the floor?"

"No, definitely not."

"Great," I say, still feeling awkward. "I'll go brush my teeth. Be right back."

In the bathroom, I also splash my face with cold water. Why am I feeling so nervous? It's ridiculous. And okay, I'm about to share a bed with a relative stranger, but there's no romance involved, no expectations... *So please, Nikki, stop being such a wuss and go sleep with the guy.*

Diego is already under the covers when I get back to the bedroom, and the first thought that crosses my mind is: *Has he kept the sweatpants?*

Easy to find out...

I circle to the left side of the bed and slide under the sheets next to him, casting a furtive glance at his legs—the sweatpants stayed.

"Is the cat sleeping in bed, too?" Diego asks.

"Yeah, Mr. Darcy always sleeps with me when I'm

home. You don't want him?"

He squirms a little in the bed. "It's just that he's right on my feet. I don't think I can sleep with him there."

I bend forward and gently move Mr. Darcy to the foot corner on my side of the bed. He regards me in outrage, incredulous that I would dare disturb him. But then he starts kneading the comforter and settles down without further protest.

"Better?" I ask Diego.

"Yep, thank you… So, I guess it's goodnight."

I kill the lights. "Night."

I feel Diego shifting under the covers, probably to sleep on his side, but I keep rigidly supine and immobile, careful not to touch him even with a toe, and also attentive not to disturb Mr. Darcy. I'm never going to fall asleep this way, too many variables. I stare into the dark for a long time. But then Diego's breathing becomes low and regular, and Mr. Darcy starts purring, and both sounds kind of lull me into sleep because I feel my lids getting heavier and heavier and…

***

What time is it? Where am I? What's this thing between my legs? And what's pushing me from behind?

With horror, I realize that it's morning, and I'm at my parents' house. That the thing between my legs is Diego's right thigh, and, if I had to guess, I'd say the weight pushing at my back is Mr. Darcy.

The new position is all the cat's fault. During the night, Mr. Darcy decided to expand into my area of the bed, prompting me to leave his feline majesty all the space he required and to shift toward Diego. But what prompted me to wrap myself around Diego like a baby koala remains a mystery.

I look up at him and find two crinkly green eyes staring back at me. "Morning," he says.

I make an effort to ignore how good it feels to have my body pressed against Diego's, and instantly thrash away from him, retreating to my side of the bed and sending Mr. Darcy tumbling down to the floor. I'm so embarrassed I don't even care about the indignant, *"Meow,"* and the kitty evil eye the cat throws me.

"So sorry," I babble. "I don't know what happened. Usually I'm not a hugger."

"Relax, boss." Diego smiles. "It would've been worse if you were a snorer."

"Yeah, right. Sorry anyway." And with that, I get up. "I'm heading down for breakfast. Join us whenever you want."

Even the thought of having to face my sure-to-be-angry sister can't keep me in this room right now.

Weird.

At breakfast, Julia at least waits until after my first cup of coffee to punish me for the pizza.

I'm reaching for my third slice of toast when she snaps, "Shouldn't you be watching how many carbs you eat at your age?" I'm still debating if she's calling me fat, old, or both, when she adds, "I mean, after all that pizza last night."

I stop buttering the toast to look at her. "I'm not the one getting married, so, no, I don't need to go on a neurotic diet."

To make my point, I take another generous slab of butter and spread it on my slice.

"Well, even if you're *not* the one getting married"—she says it in a nasty, *as if* tone—"you still need to fit in your bridesmaid dress."

"Are you really being this petty over pizza?"

My mom is not at the table, leaving only the male population to witness this exchange. My dad doesn't seem to care; he's used to our bickering. He's reading the paper, face hidden behind it, while Paul and Diego are doing their best to stare at their plates, pretending they don't exist.

"If you didn't like dinner, you should've just said so, instead of being dishonest and eating pizza behind my back."

"Dishonest? I was hungry, and I ordered pizza. Big deal! You want honesty? Your vegan cuisine sucks, as do all your other eating habits."

"What other eating habits?"

I start talking in a mock shrill-posh voice. "No sugar, no dairy, no meat, no gluten, no salt…"

"Maybe you shouldn't be my maid of honor after all."

"Ask another one of your friends with an eating disorder; I'm sure she'll look stunning in her dress."

"Girls…" My dad intervenes without lowering his paper, using his "enough" tone.

"Dad, she started it," I say, realizing I've successfully reverted to being a sulky teenager.

Dad lowers the paper just a few inches and arches an eyebrow at me from behind his reading glasses.

"Fine," I snap. "Take her side. It's what you always do." And with that, in true adolescent fashion, I leave my breakfast unfinished and storm upstairs to my room, slamming the door shut behind me.

Fourteen

Frosty the Snowman

When Diego joins me in my room, I'm pacing around it in circles, fuming with suppressed rage.

"That was an interesting breakfast," he says.

"See what I have to put up with?" I rant. "How spoiled she is, and how my parents always take her side?"

"Your dad didn't take anyone's side."

"You only say that because you can't recognize the subtleties. And then, what did I do, anyway? I ordered a pizza. Big deal. It's not like I forced her to eat fried chicken, so why should I eat tofu?"

"Can't you see your sister is just jealous of you?"

"Jealous? Why would she be jealous?"

"Because she spent hours cooking and nobody liked her dinner, whereas everyone came to you to get contraband pizza."

"That's ridiculous. And even if it were true, that doesn't justify her calling me fat and old. She's so petty."

"I don't remember Julia calling you fat or old."

"But she did, in female code language."

"You girls have a secret language?"

"All gals do; it's Bitchenglish. Most of the time, when a woman tells another woman, 'Your new haircut looks lovely,' what she really means is, 'Gosh, who is your hair stylist? Better make sure I never go to that butcher.'"

"And how do you recognize when someone is talking to you in Bitchenglish?"

"Instinct, and years of faring in the lipstick jungle."

Diego drops his hands on my shoulders to steady me before I dig a trench in the floor with my pacing. "Relax," he says, pinning me in place with those wonderful eyes of his. "You need to get out of the house."

"Yeah, you're right, we should go out," I agree, trying to ignore the warmth spreading from my shoulders downward. "Where do you want to go? Yesterday was pretty much the whole tour. There's not much else to do here in winter. I guess we could go to the brewery and get drunk."

"At ten in the morning?"

"It's Christmas Eve, I'm sure getting wasted is socially accepted, regardless of the hour. How else would people cope?"

"I was thinking of a more wholesome Christmas tradition…"

"Like what?" I ask suspiciously.

"Want to build a snowman?"

"What?" I step back, shrugging free of his hands. "You know I hate all things Christmas, not to mention it's freezing out there."

"Cover up, then." He smiles encouragingly. "Come on, I always make snowmen with my brothers when I'm home. It's a tradition."

I notice a hint of sadness in his voice. "Are you sorry you can't spend the holidays with your family?"

He shrugs. "A little, but I told them it was work. They understand. And I promised to go visit as soon as I can."

"Okay."

"To the snowman?" Diego asks hopefully.

"No."

"Come on, I promise the fresh air and hard work will make you feel much better afterward. Plus, what else would you do all morning?"

"I brought a book; I can stay in bed reading with Mr. Darcy. Better use of my time than freezing my ass off in the snow to build a stupid puppet."

"Right, especially if you want everyone to think you're hiding up here."

"Hiding? Why would I be hiding?"

Diego shrugs. "People with a dirty conscience usually do."

"I don't have a dirty conscience. I did nothing wrong…" I'm about to start on a tirade when I notice his foxy grin. "Oh, I see what you're trying to do here. Sneaky you."

He puts on an innocent expression that doesn't reach his mischievous eyes. "Me?"

"Yeah, you, Mister."

Diego lets all pretense go and flashes me a dashing smile. "Did it work?"

How can anyone say no to that face?

Nonetheless, I scowl. "Snowman it is. Are you equipped for the snow?"

"I have my biker boots."

"Those will get soaked in a second. I'll see if we can borrow an old pair of my dad's. What's your size?"

"Eleven, eleven and a half?"

I solemnly swear that I'm not thinking about big socks.

"Mmm, Dad's boots won't fit, then. But maybe we still have something left from Bill, Julia's ex. He was a half-giant. You have pants?"

"I can use my riding pants, they're waterproof." He fishes them out of his bag.

"Great. Go get changed in the bathroom and wait for me downstairs."

"Aye, aye, captain."

I open the door and push him out, hissing, "I'm not bossy."

"Sure you're not." Diego winks, before turning on his heel and heading for the bathroom.

I close the door behind him, then search my old closet for snow-appropriate clothing. I find an old pair of cyan and pink snow pants, and an equally old gray fleece. A heavyweight one, so thick you can go outside wearing no jacket.

I smell it to make sure it's still wearable. A bit stale, but it'll do. And the pants have a distinct nineties vibe, but I can't make miracles. If Ron Weasley couldn't conjure better clothes out of thin air, neither can I.

I swap the cat-hoodie PJs for a sweater, change my leggings, and put the fleece on. Dressed like a sixteen-year-old version of myself, I go scavenge in the garage for my old snow boots and gloves, and any footwear that will fit Diego... which I find at the bottom of the shoe closet.

These were definitely once Billy's boots; the poor kid used to practically live here before Julia dumped him to move to the city. They're not in particularly good shape, but they seem solid enough to wear.

"Here." I hand them to Diego five minutes later.

We're standing in the small hallway next to the back door, pulling on layers of snow gear: hats, scarves, gloves, boots... It's sunny outside, but the temperature is in the low twenties.

"Wow," I say, stepping out as a cold gush of air blows on my cheeks. "Refreshing for sure. So," I ask, turning toward Diego. "How are snowmen made?"

"First, we need to find the right spot," he says,

advancing along the walkway that cuts the garden in half. Dad has plowed the way until about three-quarters into the backyard, leaving only the last stretch untouched. "Here." Diego stops near the giant hemlock that towers over the garden. "We should build it under the shade of this tree so it doesn't melt right away."

I'm thinking that in this freezing cold, we could build our snowman in the sunniest spot and still it wouldn't melt, but I don't comment.

"I'm going to make the bigger body snowball," Diego instructs. "And you can work on the chest ball."

"Okay, show me what to do."

He gathers some fresh snow in his hands and starts compacting it into a ball. When the globe is big enough, he starts rolling it on the ground, making it bigger and bigger. I imitate him and come up with a decent-sized, if not as perfectly round, sphere. Diego adjusts the misshapen bits, and then puts my ball on top of his.

"I'll make the head," he says. "Can you find some twigs for the arms and something to make the eyes and the mouth?"

I move into the wood shack to scavenge the twigs, collect two small pinecones for the eyes, and strip a curvy line of bark off a log to use for the mouth.

"Perfect," Diego says, assessing the final result. "We just need a carrot for the nose."

"I'll go ask Mom for one."

I jog back to the house, and I'm about to enter the kitchen when I overhear my mom and sister talking, so I stop just behind the open door.

"They look cute," Mom says.

"They look weird," Julia hisses.

"What do you mean, 'weird?'"

"Come on, he's not her type at all. No stable job, probably no education, dark hair... Nikki prefers blonds."

Mostly true, but how dare she?

"Oh, honey... love is blind," my mom sighs. "You can't control who you fall for."

"Love, sure," Julia snaps.

"What do you have against Diego?"

"Nothing, he's absolutely fine. But doesn't it seem strange to you that out of the blue"—she snaps her fingers—"Nikki suddenly has a boyfriend no one has ever seen or heard of, and suddenly she's bringing the guy home for Christmas?"

"What are you suggesting?"

"I don't know. Maybe she didn't want to be the single older sister for yet another year, and she asked a friend to do her a favor. I mean, it must be hard for her with me getting married before her..."

It takes all of my willpower not to go in there and strangle Julia on the spot. I don't need anyone's pity, and especially not hers, thank you very much. And what she's saying stings even more—not only because it's true that Diego is not my boyfriend, but more so because he isn't even a friend. He's just a guy I'm paying five thousand dollars to pretend he likes me.

"Don't be silly, Jules," my mom says. "They're not friends. Have you seen the way he looks at her?"

What? How does he look at me?

"No," Julia says, echoing my thoughts. "Does he have a special look?"

"Yes, he stares at your sister the way your father used to look at me when we were young."

"Mom, that's absurd." Unfortunately, I agree with my sister here. "And Dad still looks at you that way."

"True." Mom giggles. "And trust me, love, I can tell when a young man is in love."

"Mom, I think you want to see Nikki married off so much that you've put your pink glasses on and are ready to swallow whatever bullshit she feeds you."

"Don't swear, dear, it's not becoming for a bride. And don't treat me like an old lady who doesn't understand how the world works anymore. With age comes wisdom, and I can see a lot more than you think."

"I don't know. I'm not convinced. Have you even seen them kiss, like, ever?"

"Maybe they're just private people. Look how cute they are… they're building a snowman. When did you ever see Nikki build a snowman?"

I can't see what my mom's doing, but I can imagine her pointing out the kitchen window to the backyard.

"Where's Nikki?" Julia asks, alarmed.

With the speed of the best undercover agents, I quickly backtrack to the rear door, slam it shut with a loud bang, and call, "Mom? Are you inside?"

"In the kitchen, baby," she shouts back.

I walk in, plastering a big, fake smile on my lips. My heart is still beating super fast. "Can you gals spare a carrot?" I say, struggling to keep my voice even. "We need a nose for our frosty man."

"Sure, honey," she says a bit over-brightly. "You want it peeled?"

"No, I'm sure Frosty won't mind."

Despite my best efforts, I can't bring myself to meet Julia's eyes. I take the carrot from Mom and hurry back outside as quickly as I can.

"Here's your carrot," I snap to Diego.

"Whoa, what happened to you?" He stops leveling the main body snowball and gets up from his crouch. "You went inside a cute, hopping bunny and came out a roaring tiger."

"My stupid sister is putting weird ideas into my mom's head."

He sticks the carrot in the middle of the head ball, making our masterpiece complete. "What weird ideas?"

"Like we're not together, and you're really just a friend doing me a favor pretending to be my boyfriend."

Diego flashes me his impossibly sexy grin. "How absurd."

Out of the corner of my eye, I catch two heads staring from the kitchen window. Panicking, I quickly grab Diego by the hips and pull him toward me.

"And what's happening now?" he asks, the smile never leaving his face.

"They're spying on us from inside the house. We need to appear... mmm... affectionate."

"Mmm, boss, is it just me?" Diego taunts me. "Or are you taking the opportunity to discretely grope my *assets?*"

Accurate, unfortunately. My hands are wrapped around his lower back, well within ass-groping territory.

"Sorry," I say. "Emergency situations call for extreme measures."

"In that case..."

And with a devilish sparkle in his eyes, he lowers his hands on my back to return the favor.

I scowl, although I'm not at all convinced I don't like the close contact.

"Want to know what I think, boss?"

"No."

"I think there's a much better way of convincing your mom and sister we're legit than discreetly groping each other's assets in the backyard."

"What way?"

"You should kiss me."

If the cold hasn't turned my cheeks bright red already, they sure are now. "I-I should... what?"

Diego stares up at the sky. "I mean, we're not standing under the mistletoe or anything." He looks back at me, his eyes teasing. Is he flirting with me? Or is he just a really good actor? "But we should make an exception; extreme circumstances and all..." He pulls me closer.

"I'm not forcing you to kiss me," I say. "It wasn't in our contract, and I promised you no physical interactions, and—"

"Nikki," he interrupts. He's never said my name with such intensity. "Shut up."

And to make sure I do, he presses his lips onto mine. And it's no stage kiss. There's tongue, and there's heat. So much heat I'm afraid poor Frosty will melt after all.

Gosh, how long has it been since someone kissed me like this? Has anyone *ever* kissed me like this? I can't remember... Right now I can't remember anything; my brain is melting, and my knees are turning into a wobbly mess. I remove my hands from his butt and wrap them around his neck—to pull him closer, or to support myself, I'm not sure.

"Err-emm," someone clears his throat behind us.

I quickly detach myself from Diego and turn around to find Dad staring at us from the backyard threshold, arms severely crossed over his chest.

"Lunch is ready," he announces.

Oh my goodness! I can't believe my dad just did that! Worse than when I was a teenager and he would signal my date that making out time was over by turning on the porch lights.

"Guess they bought the show." Diego winks at me and affectionately pats my rear end before preceding me into the house.

So it was all just for show?

I can't help but feel disappointed as I follow him inside.

But for the rest of the day, Diego keeps throwing me flirty stares, which I find myself willingly reciprocating. What's happening to us? What's happening to *me?*

I feel different. I don't hate Christmas that much anymore. And I don't miss work at all. And whenever I stare at Paul and Julia together, I no longer feel a stab through the heart.

Today has been so weird. Like, take this afternoon. Dad roped Diego into going with him to the store to get more firewood, and Mom and Julia went out grocery shopping because Mom's pantry wasn't equipped to meet all of my sister's vegan needs. So Paul and I were left home alone for a couple of hours. We hadn't been alone for that long in ages, and after only fifteen minutes of him talking about his job non-stop—as I said, he's drifted into the most boring, corporate, figures-oriented branch of marketing ever invented—I found myself zoning out more often than not. Whereas, back when we were in college, I used to hang from his every word.

Could it be that after such a long time apart, I no longer know Paul? That the man I thought I loved no longer exists? I mean, what happened to the boy who used to stay up all night discussing politics and higher ideals with me when I didn't have class in the morning and he did? Or to the guy who used to fall asleep in my bathtub on the weekends because he was too drunk to aim for the couch? Or the dude who forced me to crash strangers' parties just because it was fun? The man standing before me earlier today just seemed so *boring*... Oh, did I just call Paul "boring?"

Really, what's happening to me?

I can't say, exactly. I just know that tonight I'm a lot more nervous about sharing a bed with Diego than I was yesterday.

Fifteen

The Night Before Christmas

In my room, I change into my cat PJs while Diego is in the bathroom and wait for him to come to bed already stashed under the sheets. And, I'm not sure why, but I even go as far as picking up Mr. Darcy from the comforter and relocating him to the armchair in the corner. Unhappy with the move, the cat curls up and stares at me in resentment.

"Sorry," I whisper.

When Diego comes in, the absence of the cat from the bed is the first thing he notices.

"So his royal highness is not gracing us with his presence tonight?"

I shrug. "Sharing a bed with us is an honor he doesn't bestow easily. Mr. Darcy likes to keep his subjects on their toes. Don't you?" I add in a silly voice.

The cat throws me a you-traitor stare, whips his tail in the air once, and then settles his head on his paws, probably deciding that ignoring me completely is punishment enough.

"Oh, you're such a sourpuss," I tell him.

But as Diego climbs into bed next to me, the cat drama is quickly forgotten. My whole body tenses under the covers for no reason. There's enough free space between me and Diego that not an inch of our bodies is touching. Still, there's a strong warmth emanating from his side of the bed, as if the air surrounding him was shimmering. Or maybe I'm making the air shimmer with heat whenever I think about that kiss today.

"You want to read or something?" I ask.

"No, I'm good."

"Should I kill the lights, then?"

"Yeah."

I turn to switch off the bedside lamp, and burrow deeper under the covers. "Good night."

"Night," comes Diego's whispered answer.

I lie there, with my arms along my sides rigid as a mummy, staring into the dark with all my senses on high alert. From the utter silence on my right, I can tell Diego isn't sleeping, either. Not a single breath coming out of him. What is he doing? What is he thinking?

Something brushes against my right pinky. At first, the touch is so light I think I've imagined it. But then Diego's fingers tickle mine again in an unmistakable move, his thumb sweeping over my knuckles in a soft caress. And the simple skin-on-skin contact is enough to make me experience a charge like a static shock. A flow of current that shoots up from my hand to my arm, then to the rest of me.

Swallowing my sudden agitation, I return his touch, keeping my movements just as gentle and light. Until our fingers are intertwined in a firm lock. Diego's thumb massages my palm in slow circles. I never thought of my hands as erogenous points, but I was wrong. This seemingly-innocent fondling is doing the weirdest things to me.

Our feet touch next. Just a tentative exploration at first, and then another joining of limbs.

I can't stand this tension any longer. I gently tug Diego toward me, and he doesn't seem to need much more encouragement to partially roll on top of me, the pressure of his body on mine divine. With his free hand, he cups my left cheek and... He doesn't kiss me. He teases my lips with his, never allowing them to stay in contact for long. Nibbling at me with his teeth, and kissing me everywhere—cheeks, jaw, neck—but on the mouth.

Just when I think I won't be able to stand this sweet torture any longer, he finally gives in to my silent prayer. The kiss feels much more intimate than the one we shared this morning, but no less heated.

We make out for hours. And I don't know if it's the fact that we're in my old room and have to be careful not to make too much noise or to keep the bed from squeaking, but I feel like a high school junior exploring boys for the first time.

Why don't adults spend more time kissing? Once we discover the main act—sex—we forget everything that used to come before. How good it is to just kiss. How intimate. How soul-baring. But now I'm back to being sixteen, and kissing Diego is all I want to do tonight. I'm not sure if he feels the same way, because we don't say a word to each other the entire time. But he never tries to go further than kissing, and a very chaste version of second base. In fact, every roaming of our hands on our bodies is strictly clothes-on, with no skin coming in contact except for our hands, feet, and lips.

We kiss, kiss, and kiss, until my lips are so swollen they hurt. Still, I wouldn't want it to ever stop. But at one point my body seems to have expended all its energy. I let Diego's mouth go and burrow my head in the nook between his neck and shoulder, wrapping my legs around his in a tight embrace. I fall asleep almost immediately.

***

For the first time in I don't know how many years, I wake up happy on Christmas Day. I'm smiling even before I can remember why, which doesn't take long considering I'm sleeping all over him.

"Hey." I shyly lift my head to look at Diego.

He has his arms wrapped around me, and gently pushes a lock of hair away from my forehead to kiss me there. "Morning."

I blush and hide my face back into his neck.

Last night, in the dark, it all seemed simple. But right now, I don't know what to tell Diego. We kissed. Real, non-job-related kissing. What does it mean? Are we dating for real now? Am I still his boss? What the hell is happening to us?

"Last night was…" I start tentatively.

"I know." Diego holds me closer and kisses my head again.

I'm gathering enough courage to ask the hard question—*What did last night mean to you?*—when an explosion of Christmas bells from one of Mom's favorite old songs invades the relative quiet of the morning.

My mother's shouting quickly follows. "Come on, kids, time to get up! The buns are just out of the oven, come down before they get cold… and Merry Christmas, everyone!"

This is my mom's idea of a jolly wake up call. She pumps holiday tunes at top volume on the stereo and calls us down to all have breakfast together with her famous cinnamon rolls. Usually, this treatment turns me into Miss Cranky MacGrumpy right away. I'd drag myself out of bed, join the breakfast table with a frown, only half-appreciate the deliciousness of my mother's buns, and ready myself for a day of misery spent defending my dating life—or lack of thereof.

But not today. Today, I'm ready to gorge on buttery cinnamon rolls, I want to unwrap the presents, eat the turkey, and I might even start humming holiday tunes under my breath. Not even Aunt Betsy can ruin my mood.

"Better not make her wait," I say, sitting up, glad I have an excuse to postpone *The Conversation.* "And the cinnamon rolls are worth it, I promise."

We get up and awkwardly bump into each other as I side-step him on my way to the door. "I'll meet you downstairs in just a few minutes," I tell him.

In the bathroom, I take extra care to make myself as pretty as possible without giving the impression of trying too hard. I wash my face, brush my teeth, fluff my hair, and pinch some color into my cheeks. My lips are already red and plump, so they don't need any extra pinching—a night of making out will do that for you. I'm tempted to apply some concealer under my eyes but decide against it. Julia might notice and call me out on it in front of everyone.

I hop down the stairs, skipping steps, and promptly barrel into Diego on the landing just as he comes out of the guest bathroom.

"Whoa, careful there." He catches me by the waist and kisses my temple, whispering, "Merry Christmas, by the way."

"Merry Christmas," I repeat, out of breath.

We walk into the dining room holding hands and smiling like two fools.

"Morning." I beam at everyone.

My mom immediately starts fussing around, serving coffee and placing two trays of cinnamon rolls on the table.

"Which ones are mine?" I ask.

Mom points to the tray on the left. "These are half raisin-free regulars." For me, I hate raisins. "And the other half is the vegan version," she adds for Julia.

Gosh, we're two spoiled-rotten kids. At this moment, a surge of appreciation for my mom swells in my chest. I'm an awful child. I never call, I come home the bare minimum, and always try to avoid my family like the plague. True, whenever I talk to Mom she finds a way to work my non-existent love life into the conversation, driving me mad. But I know she does it out of real concern for my well-being. I should try to be more patient with her, and call her more, and visit more often.

But this year I can enjoy all her maternal love, with no discussions. I dread the moment I'll have to tell her Diego and I broke up.

The thought hits me in the stomach like a punch with more force than I could've ever expected. To stage a fake breakup with my fake boyfriend has always been the plan, but after last night... What are we going to do? Are we still going to break up at the end of the week? Can you really break up if you've never even been officially together? Are we together?

The questions that have been swirling inside my head since I woke up, keep on spinning, chasing one another around my poor brain. I fend them off with a bite of warm roll and a sip of steamy coffee. Today's my first chance at a merry Christmas, and I'm not going to waste it roasting in self-doubt all day. *Que será, será...*

Sixteen

Santa Baby

On a whim of daughterly love, I offer to help Mom in the kitchen after breakfast, sending her over the moon with joy and a bit of shock. My standard MO for Christmases past had been to hide in my room until all the guests had arrived and get as little involved in the preparations—*ahem, and celebrations*—as I could.

Although my offer of help is welcomed with warmth, poor kitchen skills relegate me to vegetable-peeling duty. But I don't mind. The task is easy and repetitive; it has a steadiness to it that's keeping me Zen. I'm so at peace with the universe today. I even manage not to roll my eyes whenever Julia takes Mom's perfect recipes and mangles them with her new vegan creed. Thankfully, the special menu will apply only to her today—and to any volunteers. I doubt there'll be any. Maybe Paul will taste something out of sheer love—or duty.

I wait for the usual pang of the heart, or the tightening in my chest, that I get whenever I think about how Paul is in love with my sister. But it doesn't come. Zero. Nada. No pain. No wistfulness. Was one night with Diego really enough to make me forget Paul? Okay, it wasn't really just one night. We've been living together for two weeks, learning everything about each other…

A sudden rush of heat spreads over my cheeks. Oh gosh, the guy knows so much about me. Too much. Like my non-existent romantic track record. I can't date someone who knows all my secrets. I need a consultation ASAP.

155

"Mom." I throw the last peeled carrot into the bowl. "The vegetables are ready; you need something else? I wanted to drop by Blair's house and wish her Merry Christmas."

"No, sweetheart, you go right ahead. And please wish Mr. and Mrs. Walker happy holidays from us."

"Will do."

I wash my hands, put on my jacket and boots, and march across the street.

***

I barge into Blair's room. "We need to talk."

"And Merry Christmas to you, too." Blair smirks at me from the mirror on her dressing table, then turns around in her chair to look me in the eye. "Did Julia make you eat cold mashed potatoes or something?"

"No, way worse."

"Worse than when Ross says the wrong name at the altar?" She starts playing our usual game of comparing situations to things that happened in TV shows and movies.

"Worse. Everyone hated Emily."

"Mmm… Better or worse than when Ben Stiller rescues the wrong cat in *Meet the Parents,* sprays his tail with paint, and then gets caught?"

"Funny one." I chuckle. "Worse."

"Okay." She concentrates. "Better or worse than when Patrick Dempsey was killed off of *Gray's Anatomy?*"

"Ah! Dead McDreamy, that's a low blow. Better."

With a smug smile, Blair orders, "Tell me what happened."

I bite my lower lip. "I made out with Diego all night."

"Oh, that doesn't sound bad at all. Why the pout? Is he a

bad kisser?"

"No, it's not that." I drop on her bed. "The kissing was great. Epic."

"So?"

"You don't understand." I sigh. "The man knows too much."

"What does he know?"

"That I'm such a screw-up with men I needed to hire a fake boyfriend for the holidays..."

"And apparently he doesn't care; he wouldn't have kissed you otherwise... Did you start it, or did he?"

Well, he brushed his hand against mine first. And he was the one who suggested we kiss in the garden, too.

"He did, I think."

Blair flashes me an evil grin. "Was it only kissing?"

"Yeah, same as I used to do with Jackson Spencer and you with Andy Bryant before, you know, we discovered sex?"

My best friend stares at the ceiling in awe. "Those were the most romantic afternoons of my life. I don't think anyone ever kissed me like that after junior year."

"Not even Richard?"

"Richard is a great kisser, the best, really. But we never spent a whole night *just* kissing."

"Try it when we get back to New York. Last night, I was sixteen again."

Blair's face lights up. "I'm so happy for you."

I scoff. "There's nothing to be happy about. Do you really think Diego could like me?"

"He spent the night kissing you silly... Seems like a good hint."

"But he's so good looking, and we're so different. Could

it ever work between us?"

"Wait, you want this to get serious? So you're not just having fun?"

I hesitate to answer.

"Oh, gosh, are you falling in love with him?"

That's too scary a thought to even consider, so I deflect the question. "I'm definitely falling in lust."

Blair narrows her eyes at me. "And what about Paul?"

"See, the weird thing is, the more time I spend around him the less I see him that way…"

"Seriously? Just like that, you're not in love with him anymore?"

"Was I ever?"

Blair's face turns smug.

"What?" I ask.

"Nothing." She shrugs. "You came here to hear my wisdom, and I'm going to give it to you. The thing between you and Diego is great. Don't you dare go all insecure about it and try to sabotage yourself for no reason. He's a wonderful guy, and he's clearly into you. And, no, he's not too hot for you, because there's no such thing."

"You're forgetting a little detail…"

"Which one?"

"I'm still paying him to be here."

Blair waves me off. "I'm sure he'll give you the money back on the first occasion. And once you're back in the city, you can start dating like two normal people. Who cares how you met? On the record, you two met through work; doesn't matter if the job setting wasn't exactly conventional."

I stare at her still half-unconvinced, but also relieved.

"Have I been persuasive enough?" Blair asks.

I nod.

"Great," she cheers. "Now that I've got you all wised up, you want to open your Christmas present?"

***

Comforted by Blair's words, I return to the house just in time to shower and get ready for the big day. Alone in my room, with my hair still damp, I pull on the dress I brought for today: black, simple, not a hint of cheer anywhere on it.

Mmm... I stare in the mirror, unsure. My habit of dressing more for a funeral than for Christmas Day doesn't seem appropriate this year. But I didn't bring any other dresses elegant enough for the occasion. I could ask to borrow something from Julia, but would her clothes even fit me? And I'd gladly skip the chance to try one on and not be able to close the zipper. Yeah, it'd just give her another opportunity to tell me how I should cut back on carbs. So, black dress it is. Unless...

I open the closet and shuffle all my old clothes to the side until I find what I'm looking for. At the back, hidden behind everything else, rests—abandoned and forgotten—my last attempt at joining my family's festivities with any real enthusiasm.

Blair forced me to buy this dress five or six years ago. She's a fan of Christmas like everybody else and had me convinced the bright red fabric would help me get into the holiday spirit. The dress was gorgeous, and it fit me perfectly, so I bought it and brought it home to wear on Christmas Day. Then, my mom—or my sister, I can't remember—majorly pissed me off with a stupid remark, which put me off any attempt of "joining in" the celebrations. And so my dress-for-a-funeral-on-Christmas-Day tradition was born.

I take out the dress and press it against my body, studying the design. Square-cut neckline with cap sleeves, and a high, fitted waist with a peplum frill detailing. The cut of the skirt is midi length, and the whole shape has a tailored fit. Too much? And more to the point, will it still fit me? Only one way to know.

In a fluid motion, I shed the black dress and replace it with the red one, glad the zipper closes all the way up. Still, it fits a little tighter than I remembered. To make sure the seams won't burst apart the first time I sit, I try a couple of squats. Not exactly comfortable, but doable. Actually, the snug fit has the positive effect of pushing up my boobs, making them seem bigger. Yeah, not bad. Not bad at all.

I'm about to take it off when the door opens and Diego walks in. He's wearing camel chinos and a deep-green sweater that makes his eyes pop. With his hair all messy as if he's just finished drying it, and still slightly damp and curly around the nape, he's breathtaking.

Insecurities gnaw at my flanks; this guy can't possibly like me. I wish I was still wearing the black dress; I'd feel less exposed. Diego, however, doesn't seem to mind the red one. He gives me a once-over and low whistles. With two quick steps, he closes the distance between us, wraps his arms around my waist, and pulls me in for a kiss as if it was the most natural thing in the world.

So, kissing each other is fair game now, apparently. No complaints here. Still, as we pull apart, I can't help but blush and, not knowing what to say, I use the first lame excuse to avoid saying anything. "I... err... need to go dry my hair."

"Sure." He winks at me and gives me a gentle push toward the door. "I'll catch you downstairs; your dad asked me to help him bring in logs for the fire."

I nod and, still equally randy and embarrassed, I make my way to the bathroom, glad I don't have to hurry. Julia called dibs on first use and showered and did her makeup while I was at Blair's. So I can take my time to style my hair with the blow dryer and flat iron and to carefully do my makeup. I pause only when I have to choose the lipstick. I'm about to go for my usual nude shade when one of Diego's remarks about my grooming habits pops into my head: *"...You like to paint your nails in the most obnoxious, shocking colors, but you'd never use a lipstick shade other than nude. Pity, because a bold red would look killer on you..."*

I stare down at my nails, which are painted black. Not a shocking color, but still a fierce one. I raise my gaze back to my lips in the mirror. Could I really pull off red lipstick? Why not? Today, I feel like there's nothing I can't do. Only problem is, I don't own a red lipstick... but maybe Julia does. I shuffle through her beauty case until I find an almost new stick of Dior Addict lip gloss in a cherry shade.

Bingo!

Red takes longer than usual to apply. With natural shades, I can get away with sloppy technique, but with the red, I really have to be careful how I contour everything if I don't want to end up looking like a clown.

Once I'm done, I study the result in the mirror and almost don't recognize myself. Between the short hair, lips that look ten times plusher than mine, and a healthy glow that probably comes from not having spent the last few days stuck in front of a monitor—but could as well be the consequence of a night of adolescent making out—I'm a different person. Confident, sexy, and edgy.

That's exactly how I feel as I walk down the stairs. I stop with one step to go when Diego comes out of the living room, splinters of wood clinging to the fabric of his sweater. He freezes mid-step and stares up at me, wide-eyed.

I reach for the largest chip of bark on his chest and pull it off. "Be careful," I say. "You'll ruin your sweater."

"The only thing in ruins by the end of the day will be my sanity. Are you trying to kill me with those lips?"

"I thought you liked the red?"

"I like it too much." He pulls me closer and brushes his nose against mine. "I want to kiss you."

"You can't; it took forever to apply, and I don't have time to re-do it."

"See?" He kisses my forehead instead. "You're killing me."

"I'll make up for it later," I whisper.

He throws me a burning stare, which promises he'll hold me to my word.

My knees go weak under the intensity of his gaze, and I smile wider and brighter than ever before... My transformation from Grinch to Santa Baby is complete.

Seventeen

Rocking Around the Christmas Tree

The first, and least-welcome, guest arrives at noon: Aunt Betsy. As I hug her, I do my best not to wince at her usual smell of dust and mothballs.

"Nicola." She's the only one of my relatives who in thirty years has stubbornly refused to let go of my full name. "You're almost unrecognizable this year; what happened to you?" Then she delivers the first jab. "Have you finally decided it's time to find a man?" And the second. "Has Julia's engagement lit a fire under you?"

I force my eyes not to roll. "Actually, this is my boyfriend." I give Diego a slight push forward.

Earlier, after a brief moment of shock at my merry and bright appearance, Mom decided that this year I looked Christmassy enough to be in charge, together with Diego, of answering the door and welcoming the guests in. Julia is still helping her in the kitchen—more supervising nothing contaminates her precious vegan food. And Paul and Dad are tending the fire.

"Diego, this is my aunt Betsy," I use the diminutive she hates on purpose. "Aunt Betsy, this is Diego."

"*Elisabeth* Appleton," she corrects, throwing me a displeased look as she shakes Diego's hand. "Nice to meet you, young man."

"Diego O'Donnell. The pleasure is all mine, ma'am."

They shake hands and, even at the ripe age of ninety, I can tell the woman in Aunt Betsy is not insensitive to Diego's sex appeal.

Unfortunately, she recovers quickly enough from her initial stupor. "So, Diego, what is it that you do?"

"Acting is my calling."

"Oh." An evil little smile plays on her lips. "And does that pay the bills?"

"Not much. I work mostly as a server to make ends meet."

"I see." Turning to me, she adds, "Your parents must be thrilled to have both their girls settled down." The malicious glint in her eyes sends a completely different message. In two seconds sharp, she's nailed the one thing my parents don't approve of about Diego: his job.

I plaster a fake smile on my lips. "They are."

"Well," Evil Betsy continues. "I'm sure we'll have plenty of time to talk later, Mr. O'Donnell. Now, I need to go sit down. My old limbs are not what they used to be."

Oh, she's such a drama queen. She should've been an actress, too. Aunt Betsy is the most independent ninety-year-old I know. She drove here in her car, and she's never needed to use a cane to help her walk in her life. I'm convinced she's going to bury us all.

"Dad's in the living room with Paul," I say. "We'll join you later."

We watch her make her way down the hallway, spry as a bunny, and Diego waits for her to disappear around the corner before whispering in my ear, "Are all your relatives this charming?"

"No." I lean back into him. "You've met the worst; it's all downhill from here."

As if on cue, the doorbell rings again.

Diego goes to open the door, revealing my cousin Mandy struggling to keep a hold of two huge bags filled with wrapped gifts.

"I don't know you," she says to Diego with a cheery smile.

Diego is about to introduce himself when her three boys barrel into the house, screaming like crazed gremlins.

"BOYS!" she yells after them. "How many times do I have to tell you not to ruuuun?"

An ominous crashing noise is the only reply.

"I'm sorry." Mandy walks past us to run after them. "Nikki, love the new haircut, we'll catch up later..." And she's gone, too.

"You were saying?" Diego grins.

"At least she's nice."

Mandy's husband, Peter, comes in next, carrying as many bags as his wife. From then on, it's a steady flow of people: my dad's brother, Uncle Tom, with his wife Debra, their kids Michael and Sarah, who are about my age, their spouses and kids; and just as many relatives on my mother's side. Aunt Betsy's forty-five-year-old bachelor nephew is the last one to arrive at one o'clock.

There are too many people to have a proper meal all seated at the table—*thank goodness*—so the Christmas feast is consumed more buffet style. The older crowd takes over the dining room, while us younger folk claim the living room, sitting on the couch, armchairs, or on the pillows Mom has scattered around the huge rug for exactly this purpose. The kids have their reserved dining area set up in the kitchen.

There are about ten of us seated around the Christmas tree, ages ranging from twenty-eight to forty-five. Mom comes and goes, bringing new trays of food which quickly get emptied—except for Julia's special trays. All the vegan platters are still half-full by the end of the meal, scattered atop the furniture surrounding her. I spot Cousin Michael take a bite of one of her brownish tarts, and discretely spit it into his paper napkin two seconds later. But otherwise, it seems everyone has quickly learned to steer clear of whatever platters Julia is grazing from.

We make it all the way to the mini desserts stage before the questions about my new boyfriend start.

"So," Mandy asks, "how did you and Diego meet?"

"Through work," I say, keeping my answer vague, as planned.

"Yeah, you said that," Julia intervenes. "But how, exactly?"

I launch into our fake narrative. "Diego was auditioning for a commercial I was producing, and when I called him in to tell him he got the part…"

"I told her I'd rather have a date," Diego ends the story for me.

I love that we appear like one of those couples who can end each other's sentences. It's cheesy and soppy, but it's making me feel all warm and fuzzy, as if what Diego and I are saying was actually true.

Julia arches an eyebrow. "Really?"

Diego casually twirls his finger around a lock of my hair and stares right into my eyes. "Couldn't let the prettiest producer I've ever met slip through my fingers."

Okay, this is not the lengthy and super-detailed list of all the reasons he wanted to date me I'd asked him to come up with, but strangely, it's more than enough. It's the way he says it, and the way he looks at me as he speaks. *I'm sold.* And so, it seems, is everybody else.

"What was the ad for?" Julia asks.

"Deodorant," we say in unison, sharing a secret smile.

"MOM!" One of Mandy's boys—Jarred, Jake, Johnathan, I don't know, they all have J-starting names—barrels into the room. "I want to open my presents."

Mandy's sitting next to the tree. She wraps one arm around his legs and pulls him toward her to kiss him on the cheek. He can't be older than four or five. "Go call your brothers and cousins and we can all open our presents together."

"Yaaayyyy," he yells, running away.

I can't help but think, *Tasmanian devil. How does she handle three of them?*

The kids flood into the room shortly after, followed by the old folks. Those of us who were perched on the sofa or armchair leave the more comfortable accommodations to them and find new spots on the rug, so that almost every inch of the living room's floor is now occupied.

Once everyone's settled, the complicated gift-distribution operation starts. All the packages under the Christmas tree get passed around, along with the presents my relatives brought with them. We don't each buy a gift for everybody else—Mom buys the presents for the extended family circle, with one gift per family plus a toy for each of the kids. Still, there are a lot of wrapped boxes passing hands, and delirious quantities of colored paper being torn and scattered around.

I reach into the red-and-white-striped plastic bag where I stuffed my presents for everyone and start handing them out. Now I feel super silly for having spent so much time researching the perfect gift for Paul. Luckily, I didn't go too overboard with it. He's still getting a book like everyone else, only a bit more special.

I collect my family's gifts in return, and am surprised when Diego hands me not one, but two wrapped bundles. One I recognize as the ring box from the mall. The other is a mystery. I tear into that one first.

I push the wrapping paper aside to reveal a hardback copy of *Harry Potter and the Sorcerer's Stone*. I flip the cover open, and gasp at the tiny writing printed on the copyright page:

Printed in the U.S.A. 23
First American edition, October 1998

I stare up at Diego, astonished. "This must've cost you a fortune."

"Nah." He shrugs. "Found it in a used bookstore in Brooklyn. I don't think the owner realized it might have any value."

Still, I don't know what to say. I keep looking into his eyes, speechless.

He must read the unasked question in my gaze, because he leans in and whispers in my ear, "Everyone deserves a little surprise at Christmas."

Before I know what I'm doing, I turn my head to the side and kiss him. A deep, non-PG-rated kiss.

"Ewww," Sarah's five-year-old daughter protests. "Mom, they're kissing."

I pull back, smiling, and say, "Thank you."

"You might want to open your other present, too," Diego says, in a voice so low only I can hear. "Would look a bit suspicious if you didn't." He grins at me.

A minute later, I'm pulling on my cat ring when the inevitable happens. From the other side of the fireplace, Paul opens his present from me and exclaims, "Nikki, wow.

Liam Grady's new book." And then he asks the deadly question. "How did you manage to get a signed copy? I thought those were super rare."

They are, damn me.

"Oh, really?" I play dumb. "I just picked it up at the store from the new releases booth. Guess I got lucky."

Next to me, Diego tenses. He knows I'm lying; he was with me when I bought all the other books, and Paul's book wasn't among them. Let's hope he won't read too much into it.

Eighteen

All I Want For Christmas Is You

My hopes are in vain. Diego is cold and detached with me for the rest of the day. He does nothing overtly hostile, but by now I can pick up on his moods as well as if I'd known him a lot longer than two weeks. And I can tell he's pissed.

It's written all over his curt, monosyllabic answers. In the way he does his best to avoid meeting my eyes after we've been eye-flirting for days. And in the way he avoids even the slightest contact with me.

I just know it has to do with Paul and his gift. Diego is no fool, and if I got to know him so well in such a short time, the same must be true for him. But even if I'm pretty sure why he's upset, I say nothing. I'm too much of a chicken. So I let this new distance between us fester until we're both in bed that night and there's nowhere left to hide. Not even in the oppressive silence weighing down on us both.

When I can't stand it any longer, I burst out with, "Are you mad at me?"

Diego doesn't turn his head toward me. He just keeps staring at the wall, arms crossed over his chest. "I don't know; should I be mad at you?"

"No, why would you?"

"I feel like I don't have all the info here."

"What info?" I ask innocently.

He finally meets my eyes. "Mmm, for example... Let's see..." He scrunches his face in a mock-interrogative expression. "How long have you been in love with your soon-to-be brother-in-law?"

I'm *so* busted. "Paul and I have been friends since college. That's all."

Diego throws me such a seething, don't-bullshit-me stare, that I'm compelled to admit, "I thought I had feelings for him for the longest time, but I'm past that now."

"Is that why you went to such trouble to get him the perfect Christmas present? I checked the author's website. It's almost impossible to get a signed copy of a Liam Grady book. The only way is to attend one of his book events and queue in line for hours, and his New York gigs are always the busiest."

True. True. And True.

With no intelligent reply to offer, I get petty. "So what?"

"You bought everybody else's presents with barely a week to go before Christmas, not giving two cents about what you were getting, but for Paul, you just happened to stumble across the release event and... what? You decided waiting in line for hours to get a signed book for your sister's fiancé was a good way to spend the afternoon? Do you go through all that trouble for all your ex-crushes?"

"No, but—"

"Is that why I'm really here?" Diego interrupts me. "To make Paul jealous?"

"No, of course not."

Diego keeps staring at me, clearly unsatisfied with my answer. Taking a deep breath, I try to explain the big mess I've gotten myself into. "Okay, fine, I used to have a crush on him. That's why I worked so hard on his gift." I cringe at how easily I'm now downgrading my previous obsession with Paul to a silly crush, but that's really all it feels like now. "And yes, he was a big part of the reason why it was so difficult for me to come home alone this year. Julia had just announced the engagement, and that she was bringing Paul home for the holidays, and I thought I still liked him, and that Julia had sort of stolen him from me, and it was too much to handle on my own as the spinster sister."

I watch Diego as he tries to digest all this new information.

"But now you're over him?" he asks.

"Yes. One hundred percent."

"Is there anything else you haven't told me?"

"No," I say.

Diego keeps quiet next to me for the longest time, and I have no idea what's passing through his mind as he stares down at the comforter. When he finally lifts his gaze again, his eyes are burning. "When did you stop liking him?"

There's only one honest answer I can give him. "The first time you kissed me, in the garden. It's like you erased everything I ever felt for—"

He doesn't let me finish. His face contorts into an almost animal snarl, a primordial expression of male possessiveness, and he kisses me, imprisoning my face between his hands and pressing his lips to mine with such passion I might faint. Thank goodness I'm already in bed.

We kiss for a long time, just like last night. But when he looks me in the eyes and tenderly brushes the hair away from my forehead, I know tonight is not going to be kissing-only. I haven't been with a man in forever, and I've never wanted anyone the way I want Diego right now. My body wants him, my mind wants him... I want to give myself to him, and I want all of him in return.

Diego has been in my life only a short time, and we haven't spoken about the future or where we stand with each other. But looking into the green of his eyes, I can't help but trust him with all my heart, with all of my body, with everything that I am…

Making love to Diego is a soul-wrenching experience. It shatters me to pieces, before bringing me back together in his embrace. We make love all night until we're both too exhausted to keep going, and we fall asleep clinging to each other.

When I wake up still wrapped in his arms, I experience a brief moment of pure ecstasy. Then a sheer terror engulfs me, making my chest clench under the pressure of its tendrils. I'm terrified that I'm flying so high I wouldn't survive a fall. Terrified, because I realize I've fallen hard for a man I barely know. A man whose ideas on the future I ignore. Is he looking for a relationship? Does he want to get married? To have kids?

Okay, maybe I'm jumping the gun a little here. But I can't get rid of the cloud of doubts circling my head even if nothing about last night feels like a mistake.

That's why I sneak out of bed before he wakes up. I'm not sure he would've wanted to talk right away, but I'm too scared of learning the answers to all my questions. All I need now is to shower and clear my head first; we'll have plenty of time to talk later. Now, I just want to be happy and cherish what happened.

Nineteen

Do You Hear What I Hear?

There's a long-standing Moore tradition I need to submit to on the day after Christmas. Since we were old enough to be safely left alone in the kitchen, Julia and I have been in charge of lunch. With us busy preparing the food, our parents can spend the morning visiting their neighbors to exchange late best wishes. The tradition originated mainly to give Mom a rest after the cooking marathon of the previous day, but also because, since we're basically rearranging scraps, it's impossible even for the two of us to screw up the meal.

Julia has been uncharacteristically quiet, but I don't mind. I'm too tired for conversation. Even if I got up super late, I'm still experiencing the after-effects of a sleepless night. And I might be unable to stop smiling, but the bags under my eyes are blossoming. I hope we didn't make too much noise. What if my parents heard us?

Another yawn turns to a half-smile as a memory from last night plays in my head.

Enough, Nikki.

Right, I need to concentrate on the practical tasks and stop reliving every second of my night with Diego. Not that what I'm doing requires any extent of brainpower. Right now I'm busy revamping the leftover coleslaw by adding more sauce and transferring it into a serving bowl. I'm sprinkling a generous amount of sauce over the vegetables when Julia bangs a metal spoon on a platter, making me jump.

I turn toward her. "What's up?"

"Nothing. It's only the third time I've asked you to pass me a wooden spoon."

Someone is cranky today. I grab the biggest spoon from the utensil jar on my side of the kitchen island and hand it over. "This one okay?"

"Yeah."

Julia snatches it rather violently.

"Hey, what's wrong with you?"

"Nothing's wrong with *me*," she hisses.

I set aside the coleslaw for a second and turn to face her. "You have a problem?"

"Why would I have any problem? Relax. You can keep smiling and humming under your breath, not caring about anybody else but yourself."

"Is it a crime to be happy now?"

"No, but you could be a little less selfish."

"Why? What did I do?"

Julia brutally mixes her mashed potatoes as she answers. "The fact that you can't even see it should tell you enough."

"See what?!"

"That just for once." She drops her spoons and points at her chest. "This Christmas was supposed to be about me. About my engagement. About introducing my fiancé into the family. But, of course, you couldn't let me have that. No, you had to bring a new boyfriend home and steal everyone's attention."

"Me. Me. Me. Oh, pooh-pooh, poor Julia had to share the attention with someone else, what a tragedy. You sound like a five-year-old. Grow up!"

"And you sound like a bitch."

"Better a bitch than a brat," I snap, satisfied to get the

last word in.

I get back to the coleslaw, but as I'm unloading a generous serving into the new bowl, the spoon slips from my grip and cartwheels in the air. I dash to catch it mid-flight, but as I grip the handle, a big glop of coleslaw flies away and lands on the side of Julia's face.

Startled, she brings a hand to her neck. "You didn't."

"I'm so sorry!"

I'm so focused on finding a rag for her to clean up with that I miss the mashed potatoes projectile headed for my face. It hits me in the right temple, sliding down my hair.

"Are you crazy?" I glare at her. "I didn't do it on purpose."

"You think I'm stupid?" Julia screams, and reaches for the mashed potatoes again.

"Don't you dare," I threaten.

She ignores me and—*squish!*—I'm hit near the collarbone.

After that, it's mayhem. I grab the first thing within my reach on the table—cranberry sauce—and throw it at her. She retaliates with a greenish vegan slop, and we keep going until we're both panting hard and drenched head to toe in goo.

"Can you tell me why you're so mad at me, really?" I ask.

"Maybe because I find it strange that a boyfriend no one had ever heard about suddenly appeared the day after I told you I was engaged," Julia yells, still panting. "And it's even stranger that he just so happens to look and act exactly like the fantasy man I told you about when I came up to your office!"

"You said you wanted someone dark and mysterious,

someone dangerous. I don't see Diego that way."

"I also said he would have to be tall, with smoldering green eyes, and full lips... Ring a bell? I said I wanted him to speak Italian, and to ride a bike. That he would have to be some kind of struggling artist, someone who lives paycheck to paycheck. And who buys cheap rings. That's basically Diego's identikit. You really failed to notice?"

"So what if I did? You're just jealous I stole the attention for five minutes, preventing everybody in the family from drooling over your one-carat ring the entire time."

"Oh, so now I'm the jealous one?" Julia brushes a slab of muck that's dripping down her forehead away from her eye. "That's rich, coming from you!"

"What's that supposed to mean?"

"That at least now you can stop being jealous of me dating Paul."

The accusation hurts like a slap. "Why would I be jealous of you dating Paul?"

"Oh, please. I've always known you had a thing for him."

I freeze at that. My first instinct is to deny it, but an irrational rage takes over and, calm as a snake before it attacks, I hiss, "So why did you go out with him if you knew?"

Julia lowers her eyes, looking momentarily guilty, before her usual flippancy is back. She shrugs, and says, "I liked him."

That could be it: she saw something she liked and took it, no matter whose feelings she had to trample in the process. But that fraction-of-a-second guilty stare gave her away.

I narrow my eyes at her. "Did you go out with Paul specifically to piss me off?"

"Don't be ridiculous." She waves dismissively, but I see how she flares her nostrils, like she does whenever she's lying.

"You're lying." The realization hits me in the gut like a sucker punch. "You knew I liked him, and that's the only reason you went out with him." My voice goes up a notch. "You're such a bitch!"

Blind fury takes over again, and I make a grab for the first offending substance I can find—chocolate pudding—and throw a handful at her, aiming for her face. I miss and hit her below the shoulder.

"Aaaaargh!" she screams. Not even trying to clean herself, Julia grasps a bowl full of whipped cream and slashes it in my direction, covering my entire torso in white slime. "I hate you!"

"*You* hate *me*? After what you did? Why?" I fling a saucer filled with cold gravy at her. A brown, shoulder-to-hip, gooey welt appears on her clothes. "Why would you do something so mean on purpose? What did I ever do to you?"

"You've always looked down on me!" Julia shrieks. "But now I realize you're just a loser who spent the past two years drooling over her younger sister's boyfriend. How pathetic is that?"

"At least I don't think Paul is plain and boring and without imagination. And I'm not marrying someone only to spite my older sister. Now, that's pathetic!"

"Is that what you really think of me?" a male voice asks.

Both our necks snap to the kitchen entrance, where Paul is staring at Julia with an unreadable expression on his face.

"No, of course not!" Julia hastens to say, panic written all over her face.

"And what about the rest?" I've never seen Paul so eerily calm. "Did you go out with me just to get back at her?"

"Paul, I can explain." Julia wrings her dirty hands. "It's not... I'm not..."

Paul lifts his hands to stop her. "I don't want to hear it." His gaze shifts to her clutched hands. "Keep the ring, take it off, I don't care... We're not getting married."

Then he turns on his heel and marches out of the kitchen.

"Paul, please." Julia runs after him.

Two seconds later, the main door bangs shut. Julia reopens it and screams Paul's name again and again, until everything goes quiet. She walks back into the kitchen, her tear-streaked face red and blotched, her hair wild, and her clothes all dirty from the food fight.

"He took the car." Julia throws me a withering look. "I hope you're happy now." She looks like she's about to add something, but a sob makes her whole body shake, and she runs up the stairs crying without sparing another look in my direction.

I stand in the kitchen breathing heavily, still shocked everything I just learned. A blob of whipped cream slid down from my forehead to land on the island, remind me I'm covered in food. I make a quick dash into the g bathroom, removing my pants and sweater and washing slime out of my hair and face the best I can. All the w my brain keeps racing with contrasting thoughts.

Part of me thinks Julia got exactly what she des She stole Paul from me willingly and knowingly, an

she deserves to suffer, to have her wedding canceled, to try being the single sister for a while and see how much she enjoys it. But there's another, protective piece of me that feels guilty for what happened. That wants to fix the situation for her. No matter how or why her love story with Paul started, I know her feelings are real now. Julia's stupid complaints are irrelevant; she didn't mean any of them. She and Paul are perfect for each other. But taken out of context, the conversation Paul overheard could really ruin their relationship forever if not set right.

I have to find him and bring him back home.

My mind set, I crunch my dirty clothes in a ball and hurry out of the bathroom wearing only a tank top and panties to go get a fresh change of clothes from my room. I freeze at the bottom of the stairs. Diego is sitting halfway up them, and when he sees me he throws me a stare pretty much equal to the one Paul used on Julia.

"Hey," I say tentatively. "I've made a mess."

"Yeah, I've heard," he replies, his tone glacial.

Worry wraps around me. "How much did you hear?"

"All of it."

"Diego, I can explain everything, but not now." I find the courage to climb up the stairs and walk past him and into my bedroom.

The moment I walk in, the door clicks shut behind me.

"Sorry," Diego says. "I want answers now."

"Well, now I can't." I drop the dirty clothes in a plastic bag and open my luggage to find new ones. "I have to go find Paul."

"Paul, right." Diego snarls. "Last night you swore you didn't have any more secrets."

"And I don't."

"Oh, so you just forgot to mention that I'm basically a product of your sister's imagination? When I asked you why you picked me for this job, you said it was because *you* liked me. How many other lies have you spun me?"

"None."

"Really? First, I find out you're in love with your sister's fiancé. Then, that you've chosen me to be her secret dream guy. What did you do? Did you put all her requisites in your agency's search engine and wait for the best match to pop up?"

My face goes on fire. That's exactly what I did, but I don't think confessing it to Diego now would do any good.

I squeeze into a clean pair of jeans and button them up. "It's not like that."

"So you say. Why should I trust anything that comes out of your mouth?"

Socks, I need socks.

"Because you can. Ask me anything you want later, but now I have to go."

"Because you have to run after Paul."

Shoes... where are my boots? Ah, there under the bed. "Yeah, I have to find him and talk to him before it's too late."

I pull a knit sweater on, barely hearing what Diego says next.

"Guess now he and Julia are no longer an item, everything's changed. Was this your plan all along? To bring me here to break them up?"

What did he say? I don't have time to ask him. I search for the car keys, finding them under a T-shirt on my desk. I need to go and fast.

"Listen, I know you're upset." I stop a second to look at him. "But right now I need to find Paul and bring him home. Then we can talk all day if you want."

Diego is still blocking the door, so I wait for him to step aside. He doesn't.

"Please don't go," he says.

"I have to."

Without another word, he steps out of the way, leaving the exit free. I pause on the threshold and turn back toward him. "I'll be back as soon as I can."

Diego says nothing. He doesn't even look at me as I walk out of the room.

Twenty

Let It Snow! Let It Snow! Let It Snow!

Outside, it has started snowing. I trudge my way to the rental car and start the engine to get the car warm while I rid the windshield of ice. There's a pit of anguish in my stomach. Partly for the mess I've created with Julia and Paul, but mostly for the hurt look on Diego's face as he begged me not to go.

I wish I could've stayed and talked to him, or listened to what he was saying, but right now finding Paul has to be my priority. Diego can wait for an hour; he's already so mad at me, it won't make much of a difference. I've screwed up, big time. But even if I haven't been one hundred percent honest with him, he must know how I feel about him after last night. Once the initial shock has passed, he will forgive me.

If how Julia and Paul started dating isn't relevant, the same is true for Diego and me. Feelings matter; the rest is dust in the wind.

When the windshield is clear enough, I hop in the car and pull off the road, not sure where I'm headed. Where did Paul go? He could've gone straight back to New York, but knowing him, I doubt it. Paul isn't that impulsive; I don't see him driving away to the city without a word to anyone. He must've gone searching for a quiet place to think and I know exactly where to look. No point in calling him, he wouldn't pick up.

Driving slowly in the sudden blizzard, I head for the coast. I pass a few panoramic pull-over spots without success, before spotting Paul's gray SUV sitting alone in the parking lot overlooking Harvey's Beach. I pull up next to him, get out of the car, and knock on his passenger window.

Paul turns toward me, startled. He must recognize me even through the condensation-covered glass, because he leans forward to open the passenger door for me. I hop in, glad to escape the biting wind that's whipping the coast.

"How did you find me?" Paul asks.

"The ocean. You always come near the water when you have to think. At NYU, I could always find you by the Hudson after a breakup."

Paul snorts. "Julia had no clue where to go, did she?"

"That's not fair, Paul, I have ten years of knowing you on her."

He stares back out the windshield at the dark sea. "Why are you here?"

"To bring you back home. You and Julia need to talk... Clear things up."

"Why?"

"Because you love each other, and a stupid argument shouldn't—"

"No, why are you here advocating for her?" Paul asks. "After what she just told you."

"She's my sister."

"Yeah, and half an hour ago you were throwing food and yelling how much you hated her."

"So, we fight. Doesn't mean we don't care for each other."

"Is what she said true? Were you really into me?" Paul turns toward me. "Are you?"

I look at him, imagining how differently this

conversation might've gone only a couple of days ago. "I was for the longest time," I say, surprised at how sure I am of my words. "But not anymore."

"I never knew. You never said anything."

"Paul, you were my best friend, and the timing never seemed right. Either you were dating someone, or I was, and then you moved to Chicago. Then you came back to New York..."

"And started dating your sister."

"Exactly. Until that day, I'd always thought something was bound to happen between us, *eventually*. But after you and Julia got together, I knew it would be impossible. Didn't... didn't the thought of us being more than friends ever cross your mind?"

Paul smiles an enigmatic smile. "It did... But I never thought you were interested, and when you introduced me to your sister, I took it as my final answer. You didn't see me that way, and never would..."

I stare into his blue eyes, into the life that could've been... Paul and I, we would've made each other happy. That much, I'm sure of. But that thread of destiny has been lost forever; it was never meant to be. It's another man who makes my heart beat now, Diego. And another woman who Paul loves and wants to marry, Julia. I just have to remind him.

"Maybe we should think about working on our communication skills." I chuckle. "Which brings us back to Julia. Paul, you have to forgive her."

"I really don't understand how you can sit here defending her after she's told you the only reason she and I are together is that she wanted to hurt you."

"Because she didn't want to hurt-*hurt* me—bug me a

little, yes, but that's all. I'm sure Julia didn't realize how much I cared for you, or she wouldn't have done it."

"Are you sure you no longer…?"

"One hundred percent," I say firmly. "I'm in love with Diego." The ease with which the words came out of my mouth surprises me. Not a doubt in my mind about their truth. "And you're in love with my sister."

Paul scoffs. "Yeah, for all the good that will do me. Seems clear she doesn't really love me; that our entire relationship is a big, fat sham."

"Paul, it doesn't matter how it started. If Julia really only wanted to annoy me, she would've slept with you once and dumped you the next day. She wouldn't be marrying you."

"Great, that makes me feel so much better about my future wife." Paul sighs. "I've always known she could be a little spoiled, but I never imagined her to be so mean and petty."

"That's only because you're not a girl."

"Thank you, I guess? What do you mean?"

"Female psychology is more complicated and"—I lift one hand in small increments—"layered. What she did wasn't great, but it doesn't mean she's all bad. One mean action doesn't define who she is as a person. You shouldn't punish her for something that has nothing to do with the two of you."

"But it does. We wouldn't be here if she hadn't randomly decided one day to piss off her sister."

"But does it really matter?"

"Shouldn't it?"

"Not really. How many times do people get together for all the wrong reasons? Is dating a guy because you saw him in a bar and found him attractive really any better or more profound?"

"No idea; I don't date many guys."

I playfully swat him. "Come on, you know what I mean. First dates are superficial and meaningless most of the time. It's what comes later that matters. Julia is in love with you, and you're in love with her. The rest, you can work out."

"Even if I'm plain and boring?"

"Oh, you know Julia, my sister doesn't mean half the things that come out of her mouth."

"So, Jules doesn't really want to date a tall biker with green eyes and dark hair?"

"I guarantee you she doesn't. She only wants you..."

Paul's phone rings from inside the small compartment between our seats.

He picks the phone up and stares at the screen. "It's her. She's already called a million times."

Paul lets the call go unanswered.

"Please text her," I say. "Tell her you're coming home to talk. She's suffered enough."

He considers this, then starts typing.

"Why are you smiling?" I ask.

With a devilish grin, he says, "After today, I have enough leverage never to touch a vegan meal again."

And at that moment, as he makes the joke, I know he and Julia will be all right. A huge weight lifts off my chest... only to be immediately replaced by another. One relationship salvaged, but there's still another I have to mend. I give Paul a hug, then climb out and brave the cold back to my own car.

On the drive home, all I can think about is Diego and what I'm going to say to him. There are no excuses for what I did. I can only apologize and hope he forgives me.

***

At home, Paul makes the mistake of going in through the front door. We pulled up in my street only seconds apart, but as he walked up the main walkway, I snuck around the house to use the back door.

The short trek through knee-deep snow proves worth the hassle as I gingerly open the rear door and hear my parents assail Paul with questions.

"…the kitchen looked like a war zone," Mom's saying. "You and Nikki were gone."

Dad chimes in. "And we couldn't get Julia to stop sobbing and come out of her room…"

I don't wait to hear how Paul is going to dig himself out of this hole. Walking on tiptoes, I slip inside the house and up the stairs to my room with no one noticing me.

Diego isn't in my room. And I can't help but notice the space seems half-empty.

Because it is.

All his stuff is gone. His clothes, his bag, his jacket. I take in all the empty spots where his things should've been, until my eyes land on a crumpled brown envelope lying on the bed. Propped on top of it is a set of keys—the spare for my apartment that I gave Diego.

I toss the car keys on my desk and sit on the bed, clutching the envelope in my hands. I know what's inside; still, I open it and shuffle through the wad of cash. A tight pull in my chest makes it hard to breathe. Even as my face flushes with heat and my palms pool with sweat, I feel cold.

Diego is gone. The message he left couldn't be clearer. Nevertheless, I jump off the bed and ransack the room in search of a note or anything else that would explain his absence. But there's nothing.

I shouldn't have left without talking to him. No, I was right, I needed to find Paul and fix things. Diego is the one who should've waited for me. No matter how mad he is with me, running away isn't the answer.

I fish my phone out of my bag and call him.

The call goes unanswered.

I dial his number again and wait in vain.

On my third attempt, I get sent straight to voicemail.

Avoiding me, are you?

Ooooooh, but he's not going to get out of this so easily. Nuh-uh. I mean, he doesn't have a car or his stupid bike; how far could he have gotten? Not very far. I can still catch him, wherever he is.

The sinking realization that I knew exactly where to find Paul, but have no idea where to look for Diego, hits me like a hard blow. It doesn't matter. He has to be around Old Saybrook somewhere. This is a small town; there are only so many hotels he could've gone to.

Fueled by my new purpose, I march down the stairs, forgetting to be stealthy.

"Nikki!" My mom spots me the second I set foot on the landing. "Are you all right?"

"Yeah, I-I just need... Diego and I..."

"Oh, yes, darling. Such a pity he had to go back to New York early. He told us about the casting call for the big job."

At least he had the decency to cover up his sudden disappearance with my family, leaving me to explain the fight—the breakup? What is this, anyway? Doesn't matter; this is not the time to label things. My only concern is to find Diego, explain everything, and beg him not to go.

Right, finding him. Mom is my best chance at fresh intelligence.

"Yeah, Mom, he texted me to tell me. He was really sorry, but he couldn't miss an opportunity so big. I just wish I could catch him before he goes and say goodbye in person."

"Oh, he took a cab to the train station only fifteen minutes ago. If you hurry, you should get to him in time."

"Thank you, Mom!" I pull her into a bone-crushing hug and kiss the top of her head. "You're the best."

I let her go and rush back outside. I need to get to the station before Diego leaves.

After ten minutes of frantic driving, I skid to a halt in the Amtrak parking lot, not caring that my car is strewn halfway through two parking spots, or that I could get fined for leaving it like that. There's only one thing on my mind. Only one man.

Inside the station, I stare at the departure board and see that the next train to New York is at 5:15 pm. The big, round clock dangling from the ceiling says it's only a quarter to four. I've made it with plenty of time to spare. Now I just have to find him.

Slightly less panicked than before, I search around the station. The place is almost deserted. There's no one near the tracks, or in the waiting room, or in the area near the vending machines. I even go as far as checking the men's room. When I come up empty-handed again, I walk back to the main entrance and up to the ticket booth.

"Excuse me," I say to the man behind the thick glass.

"Where would you like to go, miss?"

"Oh, no. I'm not here to buy a ticket. I was wondering if

you sold one to New York to a friend of mine; he must've come here only minutes ago."

"Tall guy, dark hair, leather jacket?"

My chest swells with hope. "Yes, him. Did you see him?"

"Hard to miss; it was my only sale of the day."

"You know where he went?"

"He left with the 3:32 train to New York, darling."

My heart sinks. "Oh. *Oh.* Thank you."

"It was nothing, dear. And happy holidays."

Yeah, happy indeed. Holly jolly merry freaking bright!

"To you, too."

I walk away and collapse on the nearest bench, staring blankly at the empty tracks. Diego left. He's gone. He wants nothing else to do with me. I was too late. I lost him…

***

I sit on the bench for the longest time. The snowstorm eventually gives way to a timid, pallid sun that starts disappearing under the horizon soon afterward. When it's all gone, the chill of the station becomes unbearable, and I find the strength to get up from this frozen bench and go back to my car.

On the drive home, my head goes strangely blank. It's empty. As empty as my chest feels. When I walk into the house, I lie to my mother and tell her I managed to catch up with Diego and say goodbye. And that, no, I'm not hungry, I just want to rest a little. Thankfully, she doesn't ask questions about the kitchen fight, or what happened with Julia. I have no idea what Paul told her, and right now I don't care.

Mr. Darcy rubs against my jeans, arching his back and raising his tail, wanting me to pick him up. I oblige him and bring him upstairs with me. In my room, I change into PJs and try to coax the blood to flow back to my red toes, rubbing my feet in a blanket and putting on a pair of clean, warm socks. Then I hide under the covers.

It's a mistake.

The sheets still smell of Diego. Against my better judgment, I grab his pillow and press it to my nose, inhaling deeply. I'm exhausted, ironically, because I spent the night awake making love to Diego, and I can't wrap my head around how much has changed in such a short time. How can one person go from waking up so perfectly happy, to ending up back in bed less than twelve hours later so utterly destroyed?

I smell the pillow again, and that does it; tears streak down my cheeks uncontrolled. Mr. Darcy is purring next to me, but the sound's usually soothing effect is lost on me today. I can't help but resent the cat a little at how content he looks; he has his half of the bed all back to himself.

All I want to do is sleep, but my brain is too jacked up to let me. But as my body begins to warm up after being out in the cold for the better part of the afternoon, the heavy blankets and hypnotic purring sound start to win. Weariness takes over, and I doze off.

When I open my eyes again, there's a faint light coming in through the windows. How long did I sleep? The bedside table clock tells me it's half past six in the morning. Oh, so I was out cold all evening and night. I sit up in bed feeling slightly sick and dizzy, my stomach protesting loudly. Figures. I've had nothing to eat since yesterday at breakfast, when the world still seemed like a good place.

I sneak down to the kitchen, brew a pot of dark coffee, and eat a leftover cinnamon bun. Before anyone wakes up, I go back to my room. Unfortunately, caged up in here, my brain starts obsessing again. I'd like to be one of those proud women who can flip a switch and immediately move on with their lives after being dumped. But I'm not. So, less than an hour later, I text Diego. No reply comes. I call him once, twice, with no result. I write him an email begging him to pick up the phone. Text him again. Call.

Nothing.

There's only silence on the other side.

By midday, my depression is turning into seething anger. How dare he sleep with me and then run away the next day without a word? So, yeah, I made a mistake. I wasn't one hundred percent honest with him from the start. But our relationship became something neither of us expected, and at least I was ready to stand and face my mistakes. Like an adult would. He's just a child running away.

Or maybe it was all in my head. He never promised me anything; our being together always had a deadline. Diego just pulled the plug three days early. He probably never imagined a future for us back in Manhattan. He had a little side fun on the job while he was here, and that was it.

But he gave the money back.

It doesn't matter. It's an insignificant detail. All his other actions speak volumes. He doesn't want to be with me? Well, then, I sure as hell don't want to be with him! I've been perfectly happy without a man for the longest time, and I was a fool to bare my soul to a perfect stranger.

I only need to seal my heart back into its bunker and go back to being the rational, sensible woman I was before.

Cold, professional, detached.

Determined to erase any trace of Diego from my life, I rip the sheets off the bed and replace them with fresh ones. I drop everything in the laundry basket and take a long, hot shower, trying to scrub him off my skin. Unfortunately, as I soap up, the light catches on the tiny silver band adorning my left hand. I pull the ring off and eye the shower drain uncertainly. It'd be so easy to let it slip down the tube and make it disappear forever, but silly me, I can't get myself to throw the band away.

What is it anyway? A present I bought myself, Diego had literally nothing to do with it. I have witnesses. There are three angry shop assistants ready to corroborate my version. And I like the ring. I slip it back on. The ring stays.

What about the Harry Potter first edition?

I'll sell it off on eBay and make plenty of money off it. That's what I'll do.

I rinse the shampoo off my hair with a vengeance and step out of the shower.

Wrapped in a towel, I brace my hands on the sink and give myself a little motivational speech, reminding myself I'm a strong, independent woman. So that by the time Mom calls everyone down for lunch, I'm a logical, put-together person again.

Throughout the meal, I notice Julia seeking to catch my eye, but I stubbornly avoid her gaze. Sooner or later, we'll have to talk. A food fight can't be our last interaction. But it's not a conversation I'm looking forward to having. What I said to Paul is true—one bad action doesn't make her a bad person. But still, the thought that one of the people who should always have my back was out to get me instead is unsettling.

Oh, come on, get off your high horse, a little voice inside my head sneers. *You were just as bad when you picked out a fake boyfriend specifically to make Julia jealous.*

I shut my annoying conscience off and excuse myself as soon as I'm done eating. My plan is to spend the rest of today and tomorrow holed up in my room, working, until on Saturday I can finally go back to my real life and to sanity. As far away from family drama and fake-boyfriends-turned-real-runaway-boyfriends as I can.

Twenty-one

Silent Nights

I've barely sat down at the desk in my bedroom, ready to fire up my laptop, when a knock on my door disrupts my plan of isolating myself from the world for the foreseeable future.

"Yeah?" I call.

Julia walks in, the image of a repentant sister. "Can we talk?"

Well, we had to face off at some point. Better to just rip off the Band-Aid, I guess. I'll still have plenty of time to be alone. The rest of my life, actually.

"Sure." I shrug and shift my chair so that it's facing her.

Julia sits at the foot of the bed. "Let me start by saying I know I can be petty and insufferable at times, and that I'm aware I have a serious problem with not being the center of everyone's attention."

My mouth dangles open. I'm shocked. This is the first time in twenty-eight years I've heard Julia admit she has flaws, and that she isn't always one hundred percent right about everything.

I narrow my eyes at her. "Who are you, and what did you do with my sister?"

"Why did you run after Paul to save my ass yesterday?" she asks, ignoring my joke. "After the way I treated you."

"Because I know Paul; never let something fester with him. He needed to hear the other side of the story, and that couldn't come from you, not while he was still so mad. Also..." I pause here, undecided if I should say what I'm really thinking. But if we have to have one big, clarifying talk, it wouldn't make sense to leave my hurt feelings out. "…I'm not in the business of ruining the lives of the people I love on purpose."

Tears well in Julia's eyes. "I never meant to ruin your life or hurt you."

"Really? Because dating a guy only because you knew I liked him seems like a pretty good way to achieve exactly that."

"When I said 'yes' to that first date with Paul, I did it only to annoy you a little. I thought we would've gone out once, flirted some, and then the fling would die there. I wasn't prepared to fall in love with him so completely after only one date. And after that, I didn't have the strength to call it off because of you. And I hated myself for putting an even bigger wedge between us. In the past two years, you've become even colder and more detached."

"Well, can you blame me? And why did you want to annoy me so badly in the first place, anyway?"

"Because I wanted you to pay attention to me. For twenty-six years, you never so much as—"

"Please, Julia, not the neglected sister act again," I interrupt. "I've always been there for you when you needed me."

"Technically, yes, but was it out of duty, or because you wanted to? I always felt like the sister you were stuck with, as opposed to the sister you wanted, or…" Julia stares out the window across the street. "…the sister you chose."

I follow her gaze to Blair's house. "Is this about Blair again? Julia, I can have a best friend and still love my sister. The two are not mutually exclusive."

"Yeah, but since we were kids, you two have always

shoved me to the sidelines of your cool lives."

That's such a distorted view of reality, I'm appalled. "Julia, I hate to break it to you, but teenagers don't like to hang out with younger kids. Two years might seem like a short gap, but it's not when you're in high school. And I'm not saying it was very mature of me or right not to spend time with my little sister, but it's the way teenage girls act. And Blair and I were never such cool kids; you've always been more popular than us, even when we were seniors and you were just a sophomore. You were Prom Queen, for goodness' sake!" I take a breath. "Plus, I don't share parents with Blair, which makes it a lot easier to be around her."

"Why?"

"Because whenever I look at Blair, I don't feel like I got the shallow end of the gene pool."

"Meaning?"

"Meaning you got Mom's blonde hair, the better looks, the bubbly personality... I've always been the shy introvert, and it didn't help that whatever I did, you had to go and prove you could do better. Ballet as kids, swimming in high school, life in New York, and then Paul."

"I didn't do it to prove I was better, I did it to prove I was worthy. That we could be friends, that we liked the same things."

That shuts me up all right. "I never saw it that way," I confess. "I've always assumed you were competing with me."

"No. And, Nik, you didn't get the shallow end of the gene pool. You have bigger boobs..." *And a bigger ass,* I comment inside my head. "...and you won't believe how much I envy your dark, straight hair. I hate my golden curls."

"That's the stupidest thing I've ever heard. You're a natural blonde; half the women on the planet would kill for hair like yours, including me."

Julia grimaces. "Guess we're hard-wired to want what we don't have."

"Are you really saying you've never wanted to compete with me?"

Julia smirks. "Maybe a little, but everything I did was mostly to impress you."

I stare at my sister as if I'm seeing her for the first time.

"Wow, we should've had this conversation ages ago."

"I know. And I'm sorry for everything…"

"Me, too."

"Well, you did nothing wrong, whereas with Paul… I screwed up big time. But I'm so happy you're over him now. And I'm also over the moon for you and Diego."

A small knife jacks its way into my heart at the mention of Diego's name.

"Are you?"

"Yeah, I was so relieved when you brought him home." Julia chuckles. "I mean, I was also a little jealous, to be honest, because he's really a guy out of a fantasy. I even went as far as accusing you of not really being together, and of having brought home a friend to play your fake boyfriend just to steal my thunder… How absurd."

"Ha, ha, ha…" I chuckle along with her. "Crazy, right?"

"But Mom made me see how much you two love each other."

The knife in my heart twists, and the wound I've been trying so hard to seal starts bleeding again.

"I hope he gets that job in New York," Julia continues.

"And we should all go out to dinner once we're back in the city."

"That would be wonderful."

I don't have the strength to tell her Diego and I are over, finished, caput. Once the scar is a little more healed, I'll come up with a credible breakup story. I can't deal with the unavoidable family's sympathy that would follow such a revelation; not in person, at least. Better to break the news to my parents over the phone once I'm safely back in Manhattan. And I can go out with Julia in the city, and lie to her for the last time, as soon as I'm a little better. But not today, not this week, not when the memory of Diego's lips on my skin is still so fresh…

"Sisterly hug?" Julia gets up, stretching her arms wide and bringing me out of my mental reverie.

I lift my butt from the chair and pull her into a tight hug. "Love you," I whisper.

"I love you, too," she replies, choked.

We hang on to each other for the longest time, closer than we've been in years. If nothing else, something good came out of this dreadful holiday break.

***

After my heart-to-heart with Julia, the rest of my stay at home passes rather uneventfully. I try my best not to think about Diego, even if every time I catch sight of the snowman adorning our backyard, it's like a million arrows puncture my chest at once.

Diego really picked the perfect spot; the damn thing is not going to melt, ever. It'll probably still be there come spring. More than once, I'm tempted to march outside and kick the wretched thing back to powder. But then I'd have to explain to my family why I've suddenly turned into a snowman-killing maniac. So I just cope by avoiding the windows that overlook the backyard.

During the day, I keep myself busy with work. But it's the nights that are the hardest. There's no escape in the dark and silent witching hours, when all the demons tormenting my heart are let loose. This room is haunted by the ghosts of our kisses and touches and... *I shouldn't be thinking about that!*

I hope that once I get back to my apartment, I can finally shake off every last, painful memory of Diego. We never shared a room in New York, and I'm so grateful for that now.

It's that expectation alone that allows me, two days later, to leave my parents' house filled with a decent amount of self-imposed optimism. After loading the trunk of the rental car with my luggage, I honk twice to signal Blair it's time to go. I've already hugged my family goodbye, and I'm ready to get back to New York and turn the page on the worst December to date. The new year will help with that. I'll write a list of resolutions and try to stick to them for once. First item on the list: avoid memories of a certain dark-haired, green-eyed person at all costs.

I watch as Blair and Chevron burst out of their house. The dog is wearing paw booties and looks absolutely ridiculous. But we're trying to keep the rental car as clean as we can, so as not to forfeit the deposit.

Chevron, however, has different ideas. Halfway down the walkway, she strays into the front garden, drops to her back, and rolls in the snow. If she were human, she'd be making angels. Blair drops her bags and runs screaming after her, but the damage is done. Dirty paws are the least of our problems right now. There's a head-to-toe wet mutt Labrador to transport.

My parents, who must've followed the scene from the windows, promptly come to the rescue. They help me line the backseat with trash bags, which we lock in place with duct tape. It's not the best cover job in the world, but it should do the trick.

"I'm so sorry," Blair pants, dragging a now-leashed Chevron behind her. "I don't know what got into her."

We both turn to stare at the dog, who tilts her head and gives us a first-class show of contrite puppy-dog eyes.

"I'm not buying it, Miss," Blair chides. "You knew exactly what you were doing."

Chevron whines and uses a paw to cover her eyes.

"She's good," I say to Blair.

"Too good," she agrees.

"On with you." She opens the car's rear door. "Get in."

"Oh, don't scowl at her," I defend Chevron, and scratch her behind the ears. "She's too cute to be told off."

"Woof." Chevron lets out a grateful bark and takes her seat in the back of the car. She's now the picture of a well-behaved, educated dog.

We say our last goodbyes to the crowd of parents and neighbors that has gathered around, hop in the car, and drive out of town. I can't believe this break is finally over!

Blair keeps quiet for the whole of fifteen minutes before she puffs her cheeks full of air and blows it all out in one annoyed huff. "So, I guess we're not talking about why Diego isn't in the car with us, or why you've been avoiding me for the past two days?"

"Nope, I'm not touching that."

"Are you all right, at least?"

"Super," I snap.

"That's total bullshit."

"Woof," Chevron agrees.

"Hey." I stare in the rearview mirror. "I was the one defending you just moments ago; you should side with me."

Chevron howls in response.

"What do you think that meant?" I ask Blair.

"That she is on your side, and because of that, she wants you to open up with us and tell us what the hell happened because it's the best thing for you."

"And you got all that from one howl."

"Absolutely."

"Awooooh."

When I still keep quiet, Blair snaps, "Oh, come on, do I have to beg?"

"I can't." I shake my head. "It's just too raw still."

Blair thinks for a second. "Better or worse than when Bambi's mother dies?"

"You can't use Disney parents being killed off; it's too sad, and against the rules."

"Oh, we have rules?"

"Mmm-hmm. No Disney deaths."

"Okay." Blair concentrates on the road ahead for a couple of blocks. "Mmm... Better or worse than when Bridget Jones finally gets Daniel to sleep with her, and he discovers her granny underwear?"

Despite myself, I chuckle. "Worse. That wasn't such a bad moment. Kind of cute and romantic, actually."

"Yeah, it was cute. Hugh Grant was so hot in that scene."

"Way too hot."

"So... so... so... Aha!" Blair hoots. "Better or worse

than when Kristen Wiig brings the bridal party to the Mexican restaurant before the dress rehearsal, and everyone ends up with food poisoning, and there aren't enough restrooms in the dress shop, so Lillian ends up taking a dump in the middle of the street while wearing a wedding dress?"

I laugh at that. *Bridesmaids* is one of our favorite movies. "That was *funny*-tragic; my situation is *tragic*-tragic. But, yeah, you could say I feel as humiliated as if I'd just pooped in the middle of the street."

"Why? What happened?"

"Diego and I had sex on Christmas Day." I can't bring myself to say we "made love," even if that's what it felt like. "And the next day he bailed on me without as much as a note and returned none of my calls afterward."

"Just like that? Nothing happened between the sex— How was it, by the way?—and him leaving?"

I ignore the sex question. "A lot happened before and after."

"So tell me!"

I do. I start with Paul's Christmas present, the argument with Diego about my feelings for my sister's fiancé, and our night together. Then I tell her about the food fight with Julia, and Diego overhearing that I picked him to be Julia's fantasy and not mine. I end with the second fight about Paul, with me leaving to set things right between him and Julia and coming home to find Diego gone.

"And you really don't see why he left?" Blair asks, a bit exasperated.

"No! You do?"

"Let's try on the situation in reverse. Imagine you were dating this wonderful guy, and were falling for him..."

Easy.

"...Then, when things get serious, you find out that until a few days ago, he's been madly in love with a woman who's already taken by his brother."

"'Madly in love' seems like a bit much," I protest.

"Would 'mildly in love' work better?" Blair asks, sarcastic. "Point is, you've been obsessing over Paul for years."

"I don't see where you're going with this."

"Be patient. Get back in the story: You're dating this guy, and things are going great until you find out he's had feelings for this woman for the longest time before meeting you. Still following?"

"Yeah."

"Then you overhear this big argument between him and his brother, and you also discover you're not exactly his type. That he went out with you only to piss off his brother. You're super mad and want to understand where you stand with him. But in the meantime, the other woman breaks up with the brother. So, she's now technically free and available. Now, once the fight between the brothers is over, you ask your guy to talk with you, and he blows you off to run after this other woman... What is your first thought?"

I try to censor my answer before it even pops into my head, but there's really no point. "That he still cares about her more than he does about me."

"See? Diego could've misinterpreted the situation in a million different ways."

"There was nothing up for interpretation. Yes, I ran after Paul, but only to make him go back to Julia."

"Did you mention that *specifically* to Diego? Or did you just go on one of your incomprehensible rants: Paul-Paul-

Paul-I-have-to-find-Paul-we'll-talk-later-bye?"

I want to say I made it clear why I was chasing Paul, but... "I'm not sure if I spelled it out, but it seemed obvious to me."

"To you, yes. To Diego, maybe not so much."

"Okay. Let's say, for the sake of arguing, that you're right. Diego assumed the worst about me running after Paul. So, what? Should his first reaction really have been to give up? Step aside. Run away."

"Did you two ever talk feelings?"

"No, it all happened so quickly. And then he was gone."

"So he's a little impulsive. Shouldn't you give the guy a second chance?"

"Me? He doesn't want a second chance, Blair," I say, exasperated. "I called him, texted him, wrote him an email basically begging him to pick up the phone. Nothing. He ignored me. Shut me out completely. Our night together was probably a one-night stand while on a job to him, and nothing more."

"Then why leave and not stay to finish the job if he didn't care?"

"Maybe he really had a better offer back in the city, I don't know. This isn't a fairy tale, Blair, there wasn't an evil queen who forced him to leave. He left because he wanted to, and the story doesn't have a happy ending. Happily ever afters don't exist in the real world."

"But—"

"Don't you dare say you found yours with Richard, and it's only a matter of time before I find mine. It's what coupled people say to singles, and we hate to hear it."

"Okay, I won't, but I'm still not convinced Diego left because he doesn't care. Did he give the money back?"

"Yeah, why?"

"See? He cares."

"It changes nothing. The only positive fact I can see out of this whole situation is that I won't start the new year broke."

"I don't know." Blair plays with her hair as she thinks. "Seems to me you guys are just being two stubborn idiots."

"Arrrhf-woof."

"You agree that I'm being an idiot?" I ask the dog.

Chevron gives two positive barks in response.

"Well, what am I supposed to do, in your mighty opinions?" I ask. "I already tried calling him and texting. I'm not going to knock on his door to beg him to talk."

"No, you're right." Blair nods. "It shouldn't be you," she says, and spends the rest of the journey staring out of the window, deep in thought.

Twenty-two

New Year's Eve

On the last night of the year, I sit on the toilet lid and watch Blair do her makeup as we chat. I'm not quite able to squash my resentment.

"When is Richard picking you up?" I ask.

Blair peeks at her watch. "Should be here in less than an hour. Gosh, I have to hurry." She gives another brush to her lashes with the mascara wand. "Could you please plug in the flat iron for me?"

"Sure," I snap.

I catch her throwing me a side stare in the mirror while I comply with her request.

"Are you sure you're not mad I didn't invite you to the party?"

"Blair, I'm not mad."

I'm so mad I want to strangle her.

"It's just that it's all couples," she repeats for the hundredth time. "You would've felt awkward, I'm sure. What with being the only person with no one to kiss at midnight?"

True, I would've hated it. And I also would've rather cut off my right arm than go to an all-couples New Year's party. But that's not the point. As my best friend, she should've begged me to go with her, and insisted that I go at least a few times after my every stubborn "no."

"Really, it's no trouble," I lie. "You know I hate couples' dinners."

"Well." Blair coats her lips in a bold shade of burgundy,

208

smacks them together, and stares in the mirror, satisfied. "It's not going to be exactly a boring dinner. Richard's friend is famous for throwing the best parties."

Oh, I gasp inside my head, *what a bitch!*

I get that her life is perfect, and she has the perfect boyfriend, and that they're going to the best New Year's party in the city. But does she really have to rub it in my face? Tonight, I don't recognize my best friend. Not as the kind and loving person who has been super supportive since we came back to New York. No idea what happened to turn on her mean girl switch, but it'd better turn back off quickly if she wants us to still be friends next year.

Pretending I'm busy with the flat iron cord, I turn away from her to hide my seething look of outrage.

"Cool party or not, it's still going to be a cheesy PDA shit show," I say, harsher than I meant.

"Right," Blair agrees. "I'd so rather spend the night in watching TV than having to get all dressed up and go out in the cold for a whole night of partying."

As she says this, she pulls on the expensive new dress Richard brought her from London and admires how it perfectly hugs her figure in the mirror. She doesn't look like someone who'd rather spend the night in and order takeout pizza for dinner.

She twirls around once, and then turns toward me. "Mind getting the zipper?"

"Not at all." I pull the back of her dress together and slash the zipper up in one rough movement.

"Hey," Blair protests. "Careful there, I don't want to rip the dress off." Then she winks at me through the mirror. "Not unless it's Richard doing it later tonight."

I swear, I want to take her head and smash it in the

mirror until she shuts the hell up.

"I'm hungry," I say, as an excuse to leave the bathroom. I can't stand her presence right now. "I'm going to order pizza."

I've just hung up with the delivery guy when Blair comes marching into the living room surrounded by a cloud of perfume. With high heels, her new dress, perfect makeup, and a stylish coat on, she looks one hundred percent like a character from *The Devil Wears Prada*.

"Richard just texted," she trills. "He's downstairs. Is your pizza arriving soon?"

"No," I sulk. "Apparently there're a lot of people spending the night in and ordering pizza."

"See? I told you it's the best way to spend the night." She smiles, and sighs. "New Year's is *so* overrated, really."

My eyes turn to slits. "Absolutely."

"I really gotta go now." She shrugs. "I'm staying at Richard's tonight, so don't wait up for me."

"I won't."

"Well, don't have too much fun without me." Blair opens the door and waltzes out of the apartment. "See yah."

I slam the door shut after her and lean against it. *What the hell?*

Bitch.

She made me want to smash everything in the house. I need to relax.

The pizza boy said the wait would be well over an hour, so I might as well take a bath in the meantime. I go back to the bathroom, fill the tub to the brim with hot water, and happily empty half of Blair's super expensive perfumed oils in it in petty revenge.

When the doorbell rings a while later, I've just finished

changing into one of my favorite cat PJs—about eighty percent of my PJs feature cats—and am much more relaxed.

I push the speaker button on the buzzer. "I'm up on the fourth floor," I inform the pizza boy.

"I know," a voice I recognize instantly says back.

Diego! I hate the way my heartbeat immediately speeds up. What is he doing here?

"What are you doing here?"

"Expecting someone else?"

"Yeah, pizza. What do you want?"

"To talk."

"Now? What about a week ago, when I called you a thousand times and begged you to pick up the phone?"

"I'm sorry. Can you please let me in and insult me in person?"

No, because the moment I see his eyes, I know my brain will fry and logic will fail me. No, because I've just barely started feeling like a human again. And no, because this apartment is free of painful, Diego-related memories. Yeah, he lived with me for a while, but nothing cathartic or intimate happened while he was here, and I don't want to make this place haunted, too. This is my safe haven.

"Are you still there?" comes his voice from the buzzer.

"Yeah. Listen, Diego, you slept with me and then ran away the next day without a word... That's not... There isn't a single thing you might say that will make me open this door."

"Err-hem." He clears his throat. "I have a rescue kitten here that I was hoping to drop off with you. He's sort of freezing his tiny tail off."

A cat bribe? *A cat bribe?*

Bastard!

But I can't resist; cats are my kryptonite. Or maybe Diego is. So I buzz him in.

I wait by the door, trying to steady my heartbeat, but my heart wants to jump out of my chest and run off to meet Diego down the hall. I compromise by opening the door and waiting for him propped against the threshold.

Mr. Tall, Dark, and Smoldering Hot comes out of the elevator in all black—black hair, black jeans, black leather jacket—carrying a carton transporter box with a cat silhouette on the side and cute, cat-shaped holes for air.

It might be the coldest time of the year, but I'm suddenly all hot and bothered. When did it become so hard to breathe? As Diego stops a few inches away from me, I find it almost impossible to inhale and exhale properly. The air between us seems charged with electricity, and I'm doing my best not to notice his clean and masculine scent mixed with the smell of night winds. And, damn me, the only thing I want to do right now is throw my arms around his neck and kiss those lips.

Instead, I extend one arm toward the carton box, saying, "You can leave the kitten and go."

"No, I can't," he says seriously. "At the shelter, they said I should spend at least an hour with him before leaving him with someone else. They did the same with me before they let me take him." He's trying really hard to maintain a somber and contrite expression, but I can see the ghost of a smile dancing behind his eyes. Oh, I shouldn't have looked him in the eyes. I could get lost in there, and I need to stay grounded now more than ever. "That way, he'll have the time to adjust to his new home and owner," Diego concludes.

One hour.

Can I survive that long?

Without a word, I step aside and make room for him to enter the apartment.

"Is your dog home?" he asks.

"No, Chevron is staying at Richard's for a while. He missed her over the Christmas break."

Diego nods and walks in, heading for the living room with a familiarity I don't like. I watch him move the coffee table against the wall, freeing the rug in front of the couch, and set a bunch of pillows down with the same ease as if he were at his place. I hate that I let him so far into my world.

I shut the door and join him. He's seated on one side of the rug and has placed the carton box, still sealed, in the center. From a plastic bag, he unloads a series of different items: a soft blanket that he spreads over the rug, a plastic box that he fills with litter, a bowl in which he empties a small bag of dry cat food, and finally another bowl that he lifts toward me.

"Can you fill this with water?" he asks.

I make a quick dash to the kitchen, fill the bowl, and carefully place it next to the food. With nothing else left to do, I sit on the opposite side of the rug—as far from Diego as the reduced square footage of New York living space allows.

Diego turns the carrier box toward me, placing his hand on the latch. "Ready?" he asks.

I nod.

"A word of warning." The grin he's been suppressing since stepping on my landing finally appears in a half-smile. "He's very cute."

I scowl at him and wait for him to open the box. As soon

as he does, two tiny, half-white paws step into the light, followed by the cutest furry face I've ever seen. The kitten is a brown-gray tabby, but with a streak of auburn fur that covers his nose and spreads in a small inverted triangle between his eyes. His paws and underbelly are white.

If my heart wasn't melted before, it is now. Like with Diego, my first instinct is to take the mini cat into my arms and hug the little furball to my chest.

The urge must be written all over my face, because Diego warns me, "Let him come to you."

We watch patiently as the kitten walks out on the blanket and sniffs the surrounding air.

"Hello, you," I say.

I'm already in love.

"Mew," he meows in response.

The kitty follows his sense of smell to the food bowl, eats a little, drinks, and then he climbs over my left knee to land in my lap, purring. Oh, he's a cuddler. I can't resist any longer; I plunge my hands into his soft fur and give him a full-body scratch. The kitty seems to appreciate the contact, because he starts making muffins on my leg, then curls into a tiny ball and goes to sleep.

"Seems like you two are a good fit," Diego says.

I look up, startled. For a moment I'd forgotten he was here.

The smile he'd been trying to hide before is now wide and warm and... *heart-shattering,* unfortunately for me.

"I'm in no way mollified," I tell him.

The grin now turns foxy. "Of course you aren't."

"So." I pause for effect. "What are you doing here?"

Before he can answer, the buzzer goes off again.

"It's the pizza," I say. "Do you mind getting that?"

I don't want to disturb the cat.

Diego gets up and comes back two minutes later carrying a family-sized pizza box.

He places the box in front of me and eyes it suspiciously. "Are you sure you're not expecting company?"

"No," I reply, and to justify the disproportionate pizza, I add, "I thought I'd warm some for lunch tomorrow."

So not true. Left to myself, I would've scarfed down the whole thing tonight. I mean, single and alone on New Year's Eve, a girl deserves her pizza.

I open the box and, with the aid of a few paper napkins, bring the first slice to my mouth. Mmm, it's delicious.

Diego watches me, not making any attempt to touch the pizza, but with a clear longing in his eyes.

"Did you have dinner?" I ask.

He shakes his head.

"Get the Cokes from the fridge"—I jerk my chin backward toward the kitchen—"and you can have a slice or two."

We establish a sort of pizza-truce and eat dinner mostly in silence, but not without an extensive amount of non-verbal eye communication. Not a single serious word has been spoken, and yet I feel as if I've already lost. I've tried to lock my heart behind a steel cage, but between Diego and the kitten, all my defenses have melted.

The pizza disappears alarmingly quickly, and once it's gone there's no more circling around the famous pink elephant in the room.

I take one last sip of Coke, and say, "So?"

"So."

"Why are you here? Why now?"

"There's a certain magic in the air tonight."

"And you just assumed I'd spend New Year's Eve home alone."

Diego's sexy-and-infuriating smirk makes another appearance. "I might've had a little tip-off."

I tilt my head questioningly.

"Blair called," he confesses. "She gave me a half-an-hour pep talk explaining all the reasons why I was being an idiot, and then told me that if I came to my senses, I'd find you here all alone and majorly pissed off that you weren't invited to her friend's party."

That sneaky bitch.

I can't help but smile. Oh, she got me good this time.

"Care to repeat them?" I ask.

"What?"

"All the reasons why you've been an idiot."

"No," he says. "You go first."

"Me?" My mouth dangles open. "If this is your way to apologize—"

"I've always been honest with you. You've been the one keeping secrets. Paul first, then your sister…"

I want to get up and shove him out of my house, but the kitten is forcing me to stay put and talk. "You already know everything there is to know."

"Did you really run after Paul only to make him go back to Julia?" Diego asks.

"Yes. Why else would I go after him?"

"I thought you wanted to break them off for good."

"What? What kind of horrible person would do that?"

"The same kind who would hire a guy she's mapped to her sister's every fantasy to play her fake boyfriend."

Touché.

"I'm not an angel; so what? I just wanted to annoy Julia a little."

Diego shakes his head. "And look how well it ended the last time she just wanted to annoy you a little. She made you miserable for two years."

"Well, she's not perfect, either. Anyway, my relationship with my sister has nothing to do with us. You left me," I accuse him.

He shifts his butt on the rug so that he's now sitting next to me, both our backs leaning against the couch. Diego takes my hand into his and starts drawing small circles on my palm with his thumb. "I'm sorry," he says.

"It's not enough." I try to get my hand back, but he keeps it imprisoned in his. "What if Blair hadn't called you? Would you still be here?"

"Maybe." He lowers his gaze. "I received the casting calls for the Super Bowl ads this morning. I didn't think you'd keep your word on those. Made me feel like shit that you'd still be kind to me after the way I left."

Truth is, I'd set up the castings before Christmas and completely forgotten about them. If I'd remembered, I might've had a petty fit at the office today and deleted his name from the call list.

"I usually keep my promises." I play the saint. "But a casting call is no better than a call from my best friend. Will somebody have to call you every time we argue, otherwise you'll disappear off the face of the Earth?" He smiles at that, driving me mad. "Why are you smiling now?"

"Because if we're going to argue in the future, it means we're going to be together…"

I force myself to look him in the eye. "If that's what you wanted, why disappear? I get you might've been mad at first, but why not return any of my texts or calls?"

"I've misread a situation once before," he says, his gaze open and sincere. "Only that time, I trusted a woman who told me her feelings for her ex were dead, until they weren't. So when I saw you wanting to run after Paul so bad you couldn't spare ten minutes to talk to me first, it all came back in a rush. I thought, fool me once don't fool me twice. So, rather than having to hear you tell me you'd realized you were still in love with Paul, I ran away. Stupid, right?"

"*Very* stupid," I agree, and wait for a little more groveling.

"But since I've left, I haven't been able to stop thinking about you." As he says this, he gently cups my face and turns it toward him. Diego's hands are too warm, his eyes too green, and his mouth too close. "And I don't care if you picked me off a catalog based on your sister's preferences," he continues. "I'm just glad someone in your family has decent taste; otherwise, I would never have met you."

I remove his hands from my face—too distracting—and lower them to our legs without letting go.

"And you realized all of this today?"

"No, today's just the day I realized how much of an idiot I've been… And after Blair's call…"

"You decided to adopt a cat and bribe me with him?"

"The cat strategy seems to have worked pretty well." He smiles down at the little cutie. "Have you picked a name yet?"

I stare at the tiny streak of auburn fur on the kitten's face. "Cinnamon. I want to call him Cinnamon."

"I like it."

Diego squeezes my hand, making me look back up at

him.

"So, what happens now?" I ask.

"This is the part where you forgive me and give me another chance." He scrunches up his face in a cute, irresistible, pleading expression.

"I still don't know if I can trust you not to run away at the first difficulty. We were only together for two days, and when you left I was so crushed... I don't think I could survive you leaving again."

One of his hands sneaks back up to my neck, his fingers caressing the sensitive skin just behind my ear. "I won't leave you again. I promise I'll face every fight like a man, without running."

I frown. "You expect many fights?"

The foxy grin is back. "If you keep on being so bossy, I don't see how we won't."

"I'm not bossy—"

"Yes, you are. You're bossy, and stubborn, and impossible to deal with sometimes. But you're also beautiful, and kind, and smart, and that's why I love you so much."

My heart stops. "You what?"

"I love you, Nikki," he repeats, and my name on his lips sounds like the softest caress. "And I think you love me, too."

"Really? How do you know that?"

He bends forward to whisper in my ear. "From the way you call my name when we make love."

The last ounce of resistance I had evaporates. Tears streak down my cheeks, but I can't stop smiling. "Diego, I..."

"Yes, just like that," he breathes down my neck.

"I…" I'm too choked to speak.

"Shh." He massages my shoulders to soothe me. "It's okay."

Diego pulls back to look me in the eyes for the longest time. Then he leans forward and kisses me.

As our lips touch, an explosion of cheery noises and sounds invades the apartment from outside, above, and below.

And so, at the stroke of midnight on New Year's Eve, my happily ever after becomes true.

Note from the Author

Dear Reader,

I hope you enjoyed *A Christmas Date*. If this is the first book in the *First Comes Love* series you've read, you can go back to Book 1, *Love Connection*, to learn how Richard ended up being a single British bachelor in New York, and then Book 2, *I Have Never*, to laugh out loud as he and Blair fall in love, with the added bonus of meeting Chevron as an adorable puppy.

The next book in the series, *To the Stars and Back*, will feature six-times-in-a-row Sexiest Man Alive and Hollywood superstar Christian Slade as he struggles to find a girl who's not after him just for his fame. You might remember him as Richard's famous friend from *I Have Never*. I can't wait to get started on this new novel, set in sunny Los Angeles. California, here we come!

Now, I have to ask you a favor. If you loved my story, **please leave a review** on Goodreads, your favorite retailer's website, or wherever you like to post reviews (your blog, your Facebook wall, your bedroom wall, in a text to your best friend…) Reviews are the best gift you can give to an author, and word of mouth is the most powerful means of book discovery.

Thank you for your constant support!

Camilla, x

PS. Did you notice my little Easter Egg from *A Sudden Crush?*

Acknowledgments

Thank you to my baby. You were inside my belly the entire time I wrote this book—still are. All your kicks, rolls, and flutters were very inspirational.

Thank you to Rachel Gilbey for organizing the blog tour for this book, and to all the book bloggers who participated. I love being part of your community.

Thank you to my street team, and to all of you who leave book reviews. They're so appreciated.

Thank you to all my readers. Without your constant support, I wouldn't keep pushing through the blank pages.

Thank you to my editors and proofreaders, Michelle Proulx, Helen Baggott, and Jennifer Harris for making my writing the best it can be.

And lastly, thank you to my family and friends for your constant encouragement.

Cover Image Credit: Created by Freepik